The Silent Partner

Publisher's Cataloging in Publication Data

Ruse. Volume two : the silent partner / Writers: Mark Waid & Scott Beatty ; Penciler: Butch Guice ; Inker: Mike Perkins ; Colorist: Laura DePuy.

p. : ill. ; cm.

Spine title: Ruse. 2 : the silent partner

ISBN: 1-931484-48-1

1. Mystery fiction. 2. Graphic novels. 3. Archard, Simon (Fictitious character) 4. Bishop, Emma (Fictitious character) I. Waid, Mark. II. Beatty, Scott, 1969- III. Guice, Butch. IV. Perkins, Mike. V. DePuy, Laura. VI. Title: Silent partner VII. Title: Ruse. 2 : the silent partner.

PN6728 .R87 2002
813.54 [Fic]

RUSE™

The Silent Partner

Mark **WAID**
WRITER

Butch **GUICE**
PENCILER

Mike **PERKINS**
INKER

Laura **DePUY**
COLORIST

CHAPTERS 10-12
Mark **WAID** · PLOT
Scott **BEATTY** · SCRIPT

CHAPTER 11
Paul **RYAN** · PENCILER
Mike **PERKINS** · INKER
Val **STAPLES** · COLORIST

Dave **LANPHEAR** · LETTERER

CrossGeneration Comics   **Oldsmar, Florida**

GRA
WAI

The Silent Partner

features Chapters 7 through 12
from the ongoing series RUSE.

The PENNY  ARCADIAN

Copiously Illustrated

Afternoon Edition, Price One Penny

CURTAINS FOR DETECTIVE

OUR PLAYERS

SIMON ARCHARD

THE CITY'S FAVORITE SON, HIS MIND IS RAZOR-SHARP

EMMA BISHOP

A FETCHING BEAUTY, HER SPIRIT CRAVES ADVENTURE

MALCOLM LIGHTBOURNE

A CUNNING CRIMESMITH WITH COUNTENANCE UNREVEALED

MURDERED ON STAGE
BEFORE HORRIFIED AUDIENCE

VICTIM PREY TO PRESTIDIGITATION FOUL

CASE SOLVED, SUSPECT AFOOT

To conclude his performance this evening past in a most spectacular and grisly style, visiting stage magician "The Amazing Corradino" unveiled before his shocked audience a human corpse.

According to eye-witnesses, Corradino invited audience member Detective William Wilson to participate in his act, vanishing him within a gimmicked wooden cabinet before the eyes of all present. Moments later, Corradino himself undertook a water-tank escape known as the "Hydrocoffin," but when the tank stood revealed, those present were shocked to see Wilson's corpse floating inside, with Corradino nowhere to be found.

Partington's favorite son, Detective Simon Archard, on the scene and on the trail, located and confronted Corradino within hours but could not effect his capture. Since then, information provided the *Penny Arcadian* suggests that "Corradino" may well be an alias for the brilliant and noted Malcolm Lightbourne, Archard's former partner, believed deceased. Archard himself declined comment on this speculation; however, if Lightbourne has, indeed, returned in some uncanny fashion and has enjoined Archard in adversity, the *Arcadian* will follow such a story closely, as it can only bode ill for the stalwart citizens of

•••PLEASE CONTINUE INSIDE

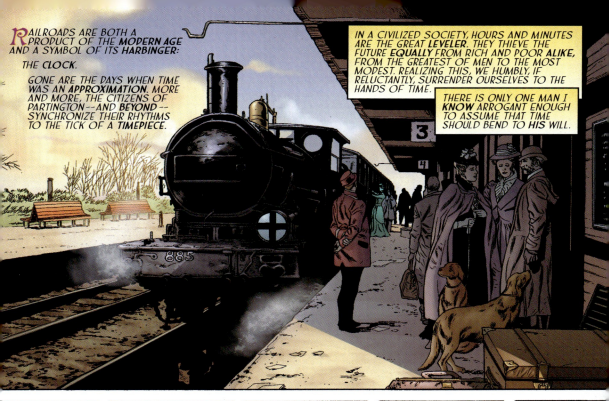

RAILROADS ARE BOTH A PRODUCT OF THE *MODERN AGE* AND A SYMBOL OF ITS *HARBINGER:*

THE *CLOCK.*

GONE ARE THE DAYS WHEN TIME WAS AN *APPROXIMATION.* MORE AND MORE, THE CITIZENS OF PARTINGTON--AND *BEYOND*-- SYNCHRONIZE THEIR RHYTHMS TO THE TICK OF A *TIMEPIECE.*

IN A CIVILIZED SOCIETY, HOURS AND MINUTES ARE THE GREAT *LEVELER.* THEY THIEVE THE FUTURE *EQUALLY* FROM RICH AND POOR *ALIKE,* FROM THE GREATEST OF MEN TO THE MOST MODEST. REALIZING THIS, WE HUMBLY, IF RELUCTANTLY, SURRENDER OURSELVES TO THE HANDS OF TIME.

THERE IS ONLY ONE MAN I *KNOW* ARROGANT ENOUGH TO ASSUME THAT TIME SHOULD BEND TO *HIS* WILL.

SIMON!

SIMON, THE TRAIN IS *LEAVING!* WHERE *ARE* YOU?

A *PENNY* FOR A VICTIM O'*FATE,* GUV? I *BEG* O'YA--

WHY? YOU'VE NO *NEED* TO.

THERE'S YOUR *PICKPOCKET,* OFFICER.

WELL, I'LL BE--!

SO *THAT'S* THE DEVIL WHAT'S BEEN NICKIN' WALLETS ALL OVER THE STATION! NEVER LOOKED AT 'IM *TWICE* WHAT WI' HIS LITTLE *"INFIRMITY"* AN' ALL. HOW'D YOU KNOW, MR. *ARCHARD?*

HIS *WATCH.* IT WAS POCKETED ON THE SAME SIDE AS HIS *"MISSING"* ARM.

A MAN WITHOUT A *RIGHT LIMB* WOULD POCKET HIS WATCH ON THE LEFT.

THERE WERE *OTHER* FACTORS, OF COURSE. THIS MAN IS

SIMONNNN!

...NOT MY HIGHEST *PRIORITY* AT THE MOMENT.

CARRY ON.

AND SEE WHO'S MISSING A *WATCH!*

I-- *CORBLIMEY!* THAT'S *MINE,* Y'RUDDY *BLAGGER!* WHY, I OUGHT TA

WHAT WERE YOU *DOING* BACK THERE?

EXERCISING THE POWER OF *OBSERVATION.*

BECAUSE IT'S TOO WEAK TO NOTICE A *MOVING TRAIN?*

A LADY CAN*NOT* TRAVEL *WITHOUT* HER *MAKEUP,* SIMON.

HEAVY OR *NOT,* YOU'D BE *SURPRISED* HOW USEFUL THAT CASE CAN BE.

WERE I IN NEED OF AN *ANCHOR...*

TICKETS!

I HAVE OURS RIGHT *HERE,* CONDUCTOR--THE FIRST OF *MANY* ON THIS JOURNEY.

WE CHANGE TRAINS ONCE?

TWICE. ACCORDING TO MY MOST RECENT *INFORMATION*--

...IT'S NOT AS IF ANYTHING NOTEWORTHY IS HAPPENING *INSIDE* THE CAR.

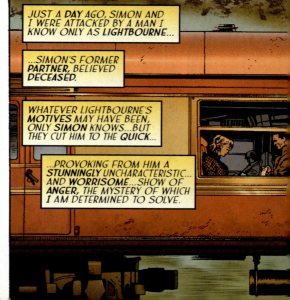

JUST A *DAY* AGO, SIMON AND I WERE ATTACKED BY A MAN I KNOW ONLY AS *LIGHTBOURNE...*

...SIMON'S FORMER *PARTNER,* BELIEVED *DECEASED.*

WHATEVER LIGHTBOURNE'S *MOTIVES* MAY HAVE BEEN, ONLY *SIMON* KNOWS...BUT THEY CUT HIM TO THE *QUICK...*

...PROVOKING FROM HIM A *STUNNINGLY* UNCHARACTERISTIC... AND *WORRISOME*...SHOW OF *ANGER,* THE MYSTERY OF WHICH I AM DETERMINED TO SOLVE.

AMUSING. WHEN I PASS OUT FROM *EXCESSIVE LAUGHTER*, DO REVIVE ME.

>HNNNNFF<

WHAT IN THE *WORLD*--?

COSMETICS.

I WAS *UNAWARE* THAT LIPSTICK WAS SOLD BY THE *POUND.*

--THE *GYPSIES* WE SEEK ARE CAMPED OUTSIDE OF A REMOTE VILLAGE CALLED *TELESTROUD.* THAT'S OUR *DESTINATION.*

AND NO MORE IS *SAID*, AT LEAST NOT FOR A *WHILE.* RESIGNED TO *SILENCE*, I CONTEMPLATE THE *SCENERY.* AFTER ALL...

SIMON MITIGATED THE DISAPPOINTMENT OF HAVING LOST LIGHTBOURNE'S *TRAIL* BY INSPECTING THE *KERCHIEF* LIGHTBOURNE LEFT BEHIND...

...ONE WHOSE UNIQUE *PATTERN* AND *STYLE* OF *WEAVING* BETRAYED ITS ORIGINS WITH A CERTAIN GYPSY *TRIBE* EXISTING, FRUSTRATINGLY ENOUGH...

...HALFWAY ACROSS THE *CONTINENT.*

TWENTY HOURS, TWO TRAINS AND ONE MOUNTAIN RANGE *LATER*, MY EXPERTISE IN *FOREIGN LANGUAGES* HELPS US COMMUNICATE WITH THE *CONDUCTOR*.

...KEEP YOUR BACK *TURNED*, SIMON ARCHARD...JUST ONE SECOND *MORE*...

...FOR VENGEANCE IS AT LAST *UPON* YOU... THE VENGEANCE OF --

...LIKE CARRYING AN *ANVIL*...

FWUMP

→HHUKKK!←

→NNNNFF!←

BLASTED *CASE!*

WE'LL WIRE THE *OTHERS* FROM THE NEXT TOWN...WARN THEM THAT PRETNARD'S *INITIATION* MET WITH TERMINAL *FAILURE*.

THERE ARE ALWAYS *OTHERS* WHO WISH TO JOIN PARTINGTON'S MOST *EXCLUSIVE* GENTLEMEN'S CLUB...

WHAT'S HE *SAYING?* WHAT SEEMS TO BE THE *PROBLEM* WITH TELEST--

DOLSUNOR!

APPARENTLY, THIS TRAIN DOESN'T *GO* TO TELESTROUD.

OSTENSIBLY.

JETE PARNUAN FILHAGRI TELESTROUD *DOLSUNOR.*

DOLSUNOR!

DOLSUNOR?

Oh, *DEAR.*

THAT'S IT... PAY NO *ATTENTION...*

SIMON, BE *CAREFUL!* YOU DIDN'T *HIT* ANYONE DID YOU?

›HKKK‹

DNN'T SWWLLOW DNN'T--

›GULP!‹

IF *SO,* I'M SURE THEY'D SPEAK *UP.*

›‹

APPARENTLY *NOT,* THEN.

TSK! TSK!

I *WARNED* YOU PRETNARD WOULD FAIL. *ASSASSINATION* IS A *YOUNG* MAN'S GAME, NIGEL.

OR AT LEAST A *CLEVER* MAN'S. AH, WELL.

BUT IT'S *ON* THE *RAIL LINE!* WHY CAN'T IT--

IT'S NOT THAT IT *CAN'T* STOP. IT *WON'T* STOP.

FOR SOME REASON, EVERYONE ON THIS TRAIN IS UTTERLY *CONVINCED* THAT TELESTROUD IS TO BE *AVOIDED* AT *ALL COST*--SOME NONSENSE ABOUT IT BEING *HAUNTED,* THOUGH I COULD BE *MISTRANSLATING.*

EITHER WAY, WE'LL HAVE TO GO ON TO THE NEXT STATION AND *DOUBLE BACK* SOMEHOW.

OR...

...

Oh, NO. *NO* "OR." THERE *IS* NO "OR," SIMON!

NO

"OR!"

IS THAT *CLEAR?*

NOT REALLY, NO.

AAAAH!

OOOOF!

WHUFF!

UNNGH!

OOOOHHHHHH

ALIVE... I'M ALIVE...

WHAT WAS THAT?

I SAID, "I'M ALIVE"--

--AND, I MIGHT ADD, PERFECTLY COMPOSED AND ON MY FEET-- UNLIKE A CERTAIN DETECTIVE I COULD--

I BELIEVE THAT WOULD BE YOUR COSMETICS BAG?

IT IS NOT A BURDEN.

♫

YOU MAY STOP PRETENDING THAT YOUR LUGGAGE PROVIDES SUITABLE TRANSPORT, EMMA.

♫

I SEE YOU RECONSIDERED YOUR *SEA CRUISE*.

AND ABANDON *YOU?* WHEN THE COMPANY IS *SO DELIGHTFUL?*

SHALL WE *WALK*, OR WOULD YOU PREFER TO LEAP AND *TUMBLE* SOME MORE?

*E*XCEPT...

...THERE *ARE* NO VILLAGERS.

IT'S NOT A *GHOST TOWN*. THERE ARE *MANY* SIGNS OF LIFE.

A CAGED BIRD...

...A CHILD'S *BALL* BOUNCING DOWN THE STREET...

YOU MIGHT WISH TO APPLY THAT *RAPIER WIT* TO THE PROBLEM AT *HAND.*

PROBLEM?

DETERMINING THE CONNECTION BETWEEN *LIGHTBOURNE* AND THE GYPSIES IS EASIER *SAID* THAN *DONE.*

WE'LL HAVE TO EARN THEIR *TRUST...* WHICH, DEPENDING UPON THEIR *LOYALTIES,* COULD BE *DIFFICULT.*

YOU'RE RIGHT. I NEVER CONSIDERED THAT THEY MIGHT BE *HOSTILE* TOWARDS US. HAVE YOU A *STRATEGY* IN MIND?

YES.

ASK THE *VILLAGERS* FOR *THEIR* THOUGHTS.

...AND YET...

...NOT A *SINGLE HUMAN BEING* IN SIGHT.

WHAT *NOW?*

WITH THE LIKELIHOOD *DWINDLING* OF AN ENTIRE POPULATION SPRINGING UP AND SHOUTING *"SURPRISE!",* I SUGGEST WE FIND A WAY TO APPEASE OUR *APPETITE* AND *FATIGUE.* I TAKE IT THIS IS AN *INN.*

SIMON, WHERE COULD THESE PEOPLE HAVE *GONE?* WHY WOULD THEY *LEAVE?* HOW LONG HAVE THEY BEEN *MISSING?*

DAYS? *WEEKS?*

HOURS. LOOK.

FRESHLY PREPARED FOOD.

FOR *WHO?* SURELY THERE CAN'T BE *GUESTS* UPSTAIRS.

I DON'T ►HUFF◄ SUPPOSE YOU'D ►HUFF◄ BE INTERESTED IN HELPING ME WITH MY--

WHAT DO *YOU* THINK?

THAT ALL I WANT ►HUFF◄ IS TO FIND A WAY ►HUFF◄ TO DROP THIS ON YOUR FOOT.

TRY DROPPING IT IN *THERE,* INSTEAD. CATCH YOUR *BREATH.*

I'LL CONTINUE THE *SEARCH.*

CAN YOU READ THE *SIGN?*

"THE *EMPTY STEIN.*"

FITTING.

SURELY. IN FACT, THE REGISTER SHOWS THAT NO ONE HAS TAKEN A ROOM HERE IN *DECADES.*

HELLO? IS *ANYONE* HERE?

GATHER YOUR *BAGS.* WE'RE GOING *UP.*

YOU'RE NOT FOOLING *ME,* SIMON. YOU'RE EVERY BIT AS TIRED AS I AM. IT'S BEEN A *VERY* LONG DAY, AND WE--

--WE--

SIMON, DID YOU *HEAR* THAT? THERE *MUST* BE SOMEONE *DOWNSTAIRS!*

OR, MORE ACCURATELY...

BUT -- THE ENTIRE *TAVERN* WAS --

-- AND *NOW* --

-- AS IF *NOTHING* UNUSUAL HAD --

DO YOU THINK THEY'VE EVEN *NOTICED* US?

NO *NEED*, YOUNG MAN. I RECOGNIZE THE LANGUAGE. IF YOU TALK *SLOW*, I'LL TRY TO *KEEP UP*.

NAME'S *OSGOLD*. TELESTROUD'S... *BURGOMEISTER*, YES? EXCUSE *KARAN* FOR BEING *STARTLED*. WE DON'T *GET MANY VISITORS* HERE.

SHOCKING. AND WHAT *DOES* BRING YOU TWO SO FAR...OUT OF YOUR *WAY?*

PASSING *THROUGH*. THOUGHT WE'D *REST* FOR THE NIGHT.

...SOMEONES.

=GASP=

I THINK SO, YES.

WE SHOULD SPEAK TO WHOEVER IS IN *CHARGE*. I SUGGEST YOU *ASK* THEM BEFORE THEY *BEAT* US TO DEATH.

OH, BY ALL *MEANS!* BUT YOU *MUST BE HUNGRY!* WITH MY *COMPLIMENTS* -- *DINE* WITH US, MISTER...

ARCHARD. THANK YOU.

IF SIMON EXPECTED HIS NAME TO *MEAN* SOMETHING HERE, HE'S *DISAPPOINTED.* NO ONE REACTS.

SIMON'S *QUIET.* CLEARLY, HIS PLAN IS TO PLAY *INNOCENT* FOR A WHILE...WISELY SOAK UP INFORMATION RATHER THAN LOSE PATIENCE AND TIP OUR *HAND.*

SO HOW IS IT WE WALKED INTO A *COMPLETELY DESERTED* VILLAGE THIS AFTERNOON, BURGOMEISTER?

WRONG *AGAIN*.

DESERTED? *TELESTROUD?* WHY I MUST NOT BE AS *FLUENT* IN THE LANGUAGE AS I *THOUGHT*, YOUNG MAN, IF I HEARD YOU SAY WE WEREN'T *HERE*.

HEH. WISH WE *COULD* JUST *TAKE OFF* AND *FROLIC ABOUT*, BUT THE TOWN CAN'T RUN *ITSELF*.

NO, SIR. MAYBE SOME FOLKS WERE OUT *SHOPPING* OR SUCH...

SIR, UNTIL FIVE MINUTES AGO, THE STREETS AND HOMES OF TELESTROUD WERE *TOTALLY EMPTY*. WHERE WERE YOU *HIDING*?

AGAIN -- MR. ARCHARD, IS IT? --AGAIN, YOU MUST BE *MISTAKEN*. NOW, *PLEASE* ENJOY OUR *HOSPITALITY*.

YOU LOOK *PUZZLED*.

ONLY AT *EVERY-THING YOU DO*. THAT WAS THE MOST UNUSUAL ATTEMPT I'VE EVER *SEEN* AT MAINTAINING A *LOW PROFILE*. WHY DID YOU *CHALLENGE* THE *MAYOR*?

...TAKE IN THE *SIGHTS* AND TELL ME THEY DON'T *BOTHER* YOU. CHURCHGOERS ENTERING A *SERVICE*...

...CHILDREN AT *SCHOOL*... A GREAT DEAL OF *MANUAL LABOR*...

Oh, WE'D *LOVE* TO. IN FACT, WE'D LIKE TO SEE MORE OF THE *TOWN*. YOU WON'T MIND IF WE LOOK *ABOUT*...?

NOT AT *ALL*.

HERE. WE'LL HAVE *HUGNAR* ESCORT YOU.

WE WON'T REQUIRE AN ESCORT.

I *INSIST*.

I'M SURE YOU *DO*. VERY WELL.

BECAUSE WE WOULDN'T BE IN ANY LESS DANGER HAD I *NOT*--

--AND BECAUSE *STAYING* WOULDN'T HAVE HELPED US FIND OUR *GYPSIES*. NOW, DO YOU MIND DETERMINING HOW FREE WE ARE TO *SPEAK*?

SO *I'VE* AN IDEA, HANDSOME. WHY DON'T YOU AND I GO FIND OURSELVES A NICE, QUIET *HAYSTACK*?

PULSFOR ACH *NUGEN*?

NOT A WORD. BUT HE THINKS *YOU'RE* CUTE.

SO *NOTED*. NOW...

IT SEEMS TERRIBLY *LATE* FOR THAT SORT OF ACTIVITY, BUT PERHAPS THAT'S HOW THESE PEOPLE *LIVE*.

THEN AGAIN, *WHO* FISHES AT *NIGHT*?

MY POINT PRECISELY.

RATHER THAN ASK THE TOWNSPEOPLE ABOUT THE *GYPSIES* -- SINCE THE LESS THEY KNOW OF OUR *MOTIVES*, THE *BETTER* --

-- I NOW PREFER TO ASK THE *GYPSIES* ABOUT THE *TOWNSPEOPLE*.

AND WE'LL COME ACROSS THEM *WHERE...*?

ALMOST CERTAINLY ENCAMPED NEAR THE *RIVER*. THIS WAY.

TENDING THE *FIELDS* BY *MOONLIGHT*. IT'S POSITIVELY *EERIE* AND --

<STRIKE *FAST!* HEADS AND *HEARTS!* *TAKE THEM!*>

THE *GYPSIES*. WHAT ARE THEY *YELLING*? THREATS?

OSSGOLD! OSSSGOLLD!

THEY WON'T FIGHT *ALONE* FOR *LONG*. OUR *TOUR GUIDE'S* OFF TO WARN THE *TOWN*.

SIMON, WHAT HAVE WE STUMBLED *INTO?* I'LL *TRANSLATE* AS BEST I *CAN*, BUT...

"UNHOLY *WHAT?*"

"I-- I'M NOT *CERTAIN*. ALL I KNOW IS THAT THE FARMERS ARE *ARMED*--

"-- AND THE TIDE OF BATTLE HAS QUICKLY TURNED IN THEIR *FAVOR!*"

AAAAGGHH!

<BY HELL *ITSELF!* WE KNEW NOT OF THEIR *WEAPONS!* RETREAT, I SAY! *RETREAT*-- FOR *NOW!*>

<BUT MARK MY *WORDS*, YOU *GHOULS*-- WE WILL *RETURN*, AND WHEN WE DO-->

SIMON? SIMON, WHERE ARE YOU *GOING?*

‹GIVE THEM *BACK!* GIVE US BACK OUR *DAUGHTERS!*›

‹YOU HAVE *STOLEN* THEM FOR YOUR *UNHOLY RITES!*›

‹RETURN THEM --

-- OR FACE OUR *VENGEANCE!*›

‹*BROTHERS,* TO *ARMS!* NOCK YOUR *BOLTS* AND LET *FLY!*›

‹-- WE SHALL *FREE* OUR YOUNG WOMEN FROM THE CLUTCHES OF THE *UNDEAD* -- OR *DIE TRYING!*›

AND THESE ARE THE VAGABONDS WITH WHOM WE HOPE TO STRIKE A *PEACEFUL DIALOGUE?* SIMON, THEIR *FEROCITY* --

WAIT. "UN...*DEAD?*"

THE *VILLAGERS.* THEIR ABSENCE IN *DAYLIGHT*... THEIR NOCTURNAL *PROWLINGS*...

EVEN...EVEN *MYTHS* HAVE *SOME* BASIS IN *FACT.* SIMON, COULD THESE PEOPLE ACTUALLY...

...ACTUALLY BE VAMP--

TO STOCK UP ON *GARLIC* AND *WOODEN STAKES.*

REALLY?

NO.

YOU DON'T HAVE TO BE *SMUG* ABOUT IT.

HAVE WE BEEN *INTRODUCED?*

→SIGH←

POINT *TAKEN.* SO WHERE *ARE* WE GOING?

BACK TO THE *INN.* EARLIER, I NOTICED SOMETHING *PECULIAR* IN THE *KITCHEN* THAT WOULD EXPLAIN *MUCH* --

WE DIDN'T ASK FOR ROOMS.

NONETHELESS, YOU CAN'T *POSSIBLY* BE *SURPRISED* THAT THEY'RE BEING "*OFFERED.*"

SO WHAT DO WE DO *NOW?*

TRY TO GET SOME *REST* -- BUT LOCK YOUR *DOOR* AND SLEEP *LIGHTLY.*

BUT WHAT IF THESE PEOPLE *ARE* VAM --

DONE.

‹OH, HÜGNAR...IT'S SO *DARK* IN HERE... CAN YOU *GUIDE* ME...?›

*S*UCCESS. THE MOMENT WE'RE OUT OF LINE OF *SIGHT,* I HEAR SIMON'S DOOR *CLOSE...*

-- AND IF MY SUSPICIONS ARE CORRECT, I SHOULD BE ABLE TO FIND --

ENJOY YOUR LITTLE *TOUR*, MR. ARCHARD?

OH!

FORGIVE THE SPARSE *RECEPTION*. HÜGNAR ALERTED US TO THE...*COMMOTION* NEARBY. IT'S BEING...*HANDLED* BY THE TOWNSFOLK.

SUCH *EXCITEMENT*. YOU MUST BE *EXHAUSTED*. HÜGNAR WILL SHOW YOU TO YOUR *ROOMS*, FRESHLY *MADE*.

SWEET *DREAMS*.

DON'T WASTE MY TIME MAKING ME LISTEN TO THE REST OF THAT SENTENCE.

PLAY *ALONG*. DEMONSTRATE *COOPERATION* FOR THE BENEFIT OF OSGOLD'S LACKWIT *THUG*.

WE WANT HIM TO REPORT TO OSGOLD THAT WE'RE TUCKED SAFELY *AWAY* FOR THE NIGHT.

WHEN, IN FACT...

...YOUR IMMEDIATE TASK IS TO MAKE CERTAIN HE TAKES HIS EYES OFF OF *ME*.

...BUT I'VE NO DOUBT HIS ROOM IS *VACANT*.

I'VE NO *NOTION* WHAT IT IS HE'S *SEARCHING* FOR...

...BUT I HOPE HE **FINDS** IT...

...SAFELY.

DAYLIGHT? HOW CAN THERE BE--

⇒SIGH⇐ BECAUSE I FELL *ASLEEP*, THAT'S HOW. SO MUCH FOR KEEPING MY *GUARD* UP.

LUCKILY, NO HORRIBLE FATE *BEFELL* ME IN THE NIGHT. I'M GREETED BY ANOTHER BRIGHT MORNING IN THE SMALL HAMLET OF *TELESTROUD*...

...AS INDICATED BY THE *COMPLETE ABSENCE* OF *PEOPLE*.

WHEN SIMON AND I STUMBLED *INTO* THIS TINY BURG YESTERDAY, NOT A SOUL WAS *AROUND*. THE STREETS AND BUILDINGS WERE *UTTERLY DESERTED*. ONLY AFTER *DUSK* DID THE NATIVES *APPEAR*...

...THOUGH WHEN SIMON ACCUSED THEM OF *HIDING*, THEY DENIED *EVERYTHING*... CLAIMED WE WERE "MISTAKEN."

SIMON?

WE'RE --

YOU'RE THE *WIVES* AND *DAUGHTERS* OF THE *GYPSY TRIBE* CAMPED NEAR THE RIVER.

HOW DID YOU--?

DURING THE BROAD LIGHT OF *DAY*, MYSTERIOUS *UNSEEN FORCES* DRAGGED YOU AWAY AND TO THIS *DUNGEON* UNDERNEATH THE *INN*.

CAN YOU TELL ME *WHY*?

SO THE LOCAL MEN COULD... COULD...

...COULD *MATE* WITH US.

NO SIGN OF HIM ANYWHERE. I KNOW HE ELECTED TO *INVESTIGATE*...

...WHICH MEANS HE'LL RETURN ANY MOMENT TO TELL ME HOW HE UNRAVELED THE WHOLE MYSTERY CLUED ONLY BY A *BROKEN SHOELACE* AND A *MELON RIND*.

NNNNFF! ALL RIGHT. SO MY COSMETICS CASE *DOES* HAVE A RATHER ELEPHANTINE *HEFT*. THERE. BUT IT'S AN ADMISSION I'LL TAKE TO MY *GRAVE*.

MEANING I'D RATHER *DIE* THAN ENDURE ANOTHER ORATIM FROM SIMON REGARDING ITS *USELESSNESS*...

BEST TO PUT ON MY *FACE*, THEN. NO POINT IN APPEARING IN PUBLIC BOTH BEFUDDLED *AND* BLEMISHED--

AND THAT COMPLETES THE *PUZZLE*. THE TOWNSFOLK ENSCONCE THEMSELVES *HERE* BETWEEN DUSK AND DAWN, YES?

YES! RESTING NEAR THEIR *NATIVE SOIL* SO THEY MAY *ROAM* AND *FEED* BY THE *MOONGLOW*-- AS *VAMPIRES* DO!

INDEED. THEIR FANGS SHARPENED BY *LEPRECHAUNS* WHILE THEY RIDE THEIR *UNICORNS* TO THE *MOON*.

VAMPIRES ARE THE STUFF OF *FICTION*. MY INTERESTS LIE *SOLELY* IN *FACT*.

THE TELESTROUDIANS *DO* HIDE FROM *SUNLIGHT*, THAT MUCH IS *PLAIN*. I'VE A THEORY *WHY*...BUT I'LL HARDLY *PROVE* IT FROM IN *HERE*.

HOW DID YOU *FIND* US?

EARLIER, I SAW A NUMBER OF COVERED DISHES IN THE KITCHEN *UPSTAIRS*--

--SIMPLE MEALS THAT I *DIDN'T* SEE BEING SERVED IN THE *TAVERN*--

--YET HAD TO HAVE BEEN PREPARED FOR *SOMEONE*.

FOLLOW ME, AND *HURRY.* YOUR CAPTORS WILL RETURN TO DEAL WITH ME *DECISIVELY*--

ONCE I HEARD THE GYPSIES LAMENT OVER THEIR *ABDUCTED WOMEN*...

...THE CONNECTION WAS OBVIOUS.

WHICH MEANS *SOMEONE* WILL TALK TO ME.

IT'S NOT MY IMAGINATION. DESPITE OUR BUILDING QUITE THE INVESTIGATIVE *RESUMÉ* TOGETHER, SIMON, A MAN ORDINARILY AS WARM AS A *COBRA* AND TWICE AS *TALKATIVE*, IS TRUSTING ME LESS...NOT *MORE*.

HE *MAINTAINS* HIS SATURNINE COUNTENANCE AS REGARDS HIS FORMER PARTNER, *LIGHTBOURNE*. I THINK I'VE BEEN EXTRAORDINARILY *PATIENT* WAITING FOR INFORMATION ABOUT THE MAN GIVEN THAT HE CAME AFTER ME WITH AN *AXE*.

A *THEORY* ABOUT SIMON'S BEHAVIOR IS BEGINNING TO TAKE SHAPE INSIDE MY OWN HEAD, BUT THAT'S A MATTER FOR *LATER*.

"-- ONCE THEY'RE DONE WITH *EMMA*."

WHAT'S PARTICULARLY FRUSTRATING, OF COURSE, IS THAT DISCOVERING THE SECRET OF TELESTROUD ISN'T AN *OBJECTIVE*. IT'S A *PERIPHERAL* CONCERN.

STILL, IF WE CAN SOMEHOW *AID* THE GYPSIES WE'VE TRAVELED HALFWAY ACROSS THE CONTINENT TO *QUERY*, PERHAPS THEY'LL BE MORE FORTHCOMING WITH *ANSWERS*.

RIGHT NOW, THE PERIL DU JOUR *IS* HHGHHPPH!

<DON'T WORRY.>
<HURTS ONLY A *MOMENT*.>

MMMMPH!

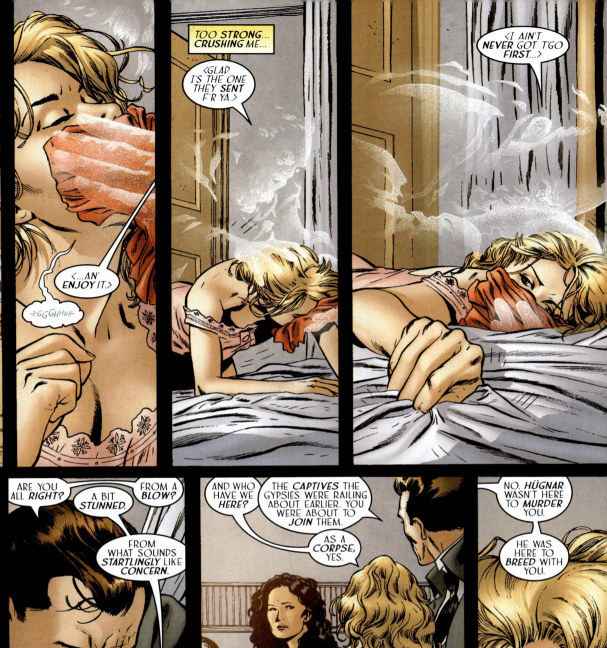

TOO STRONG... CRUSHING ME...

<GLAD I'S THE ONE THEY SENT F'R YA.>

<I AIN'T NEVER GOT T'GO FIRST...>

<...AN' ENJOY IT.>

≈GGGHHH≈

ARE YOU ALL RIGHT?

A BIT STUNNED.

FROM A BLOW?

FROM WHAT SOUNDS STARTLINGLY LIKE CONCERN.

I GATHER INFORMATION FOR A LIVING. DON'T READ TOO MUCH INTO IT.

AND WHO HAVE WE HERE?

THE CAPTIVES THE GYPSIES WERE RAILING ABOUT EARLIER. YOU WERE ABOUT TO JOIN THEM.

AS A CORPSE, YES.

NO. HÜGNAR WASN'T HERE TO MURDER YOU.

HE WAS HERE TO BREED WITH YOU.

FLOORBOARDS--! SOMEONE'S *COMING!*

SIMON, MY *POWDER...!*

AND TO THINK HOW YOU *CATERWAULED* ABOUT MY COSMETICS. SORRY *NOW?*

YES.

SORRY I HIRED AN ASSISTANT WHO *GLOATS.*

I QUITE BEG TO *DIFFER.* SO MUCH *MYSTERY* IN TELESTROUD... HOW BEST TO SHED *LIGHT* ON IT?

PERHAPS WE WALK *OUTSIDE?* SUCH A LOVELY, *SUNNY* DAY...

NO! *NO!* I--

YOU WILL *VERIFY* MY *CONCLUSIONS.*

WE'LL BE DEALING IN THE RELATIVELY NEW SCIENCES OF *GENETICS* AND *ATOMIC MATTER,* SO TRY TO *FOLLOW.*

THE TELESTROUDIANS POSSESS A PECULIAR-- AND RATHER *SEVERE*-- PHOTOSYNTHETIC DERMAL CONDITION.

SOMETHING AKIN TO *ALBINISM?*

MARGINALLY... BUT FAR MORE *DRASTIC.*

LIKELY ITS ORIGINS LIE IN SOME SORT OF SPONTANEOUS MUTATION...BUT GIVEN A VILLAGE THIS *REMOTE,* A CENTURY OR SO OF *INBREEDING* COULD EASILY DRIVE A RECESSIVE GENE TO FULL *DOMINANCE.*

...BURGOMEISTER OSGOLD. WE NEED TO *TALK.*

I--I'VE NOTHING TO SAY TO *YOU!*

GOOD MORNING...

ALL HUMANS ARE SENSITIVE TO *SUNLIGHT,* OSGOLD. IT REACTS CHEMICALLY WITH OUR *SKIN,* EVEN THROUGH LIGHT *CLOTHING.*

YOU'RE FOLLOWING ME SO FAR?

I... YES.

IN ORDINARY PEOPLE, SUCH SENSITIVITY CAUSES *SUNBURN* AND THE SLOUGHING OFF OF *DEAD EPIDERMAL CELLS.*

WITH *YOU,* IT RELEASES SOMETHING *MORE* FROM THE SKIN... QUITE *PAINFULLY,* I MIGHT ADD.

MICROSCOPIC *PARTICLES.* THEORETICIANS CALL THEM *"ELECTRONS."*

IN FACT, THE *SUN'S RAYS* CREATE AROUND YOU *CLOUDS OF FREE ELECTRONS* -- CLOUDS WHICH, SCIENCE SAYS, *ABSORB ALL LIGHT* --

-- MAKING YOU, IN EFFECT, *INVISIBLE* --

--AND *HELPLESS.*

HELPLESS?

BUT WHY DO YOU *STEAL* US FROM OUR *BEDS?* DO YOU HOLD US SOMEHOW *RESPONSIBLE* FOR THIS CONDITION?

ON THE *CONTRARY*, MY *DEAR*...IT'S *YOU* WHO'LL *SAVE* US.

WITH SO LITTLE LIGHT REACHING THEIR *EYES*, THEIR SIGHT IS BADLY, THOUGH NOT IMPOSSIBLY, *LIMITED* --

-- WHICH IS WHAT FORCES THEM UNDERGROUND BY DAY INTO THE ONE ROOM IN TOWN BUILT DEEP ENOUGH TO FULLY *SHIELD* THEM.

EVERYTHING MR. ARCHARD SAYS IS *TRUE*...BUT THERE IS *MORE*. DESPITE OUR *PRAYERS*, WITH EACH GENERATION, OUR SENSITIVITY *INCREASES*. THE CONDITION *WORSENS*.

OUR ONLY HOPE IS TO BREED IT *OUT*, BUT WE CANNOT... WITHOUT *FRESH BLOOD*.

AND GATHERING WOMEN FROM NEIGHBORING *TOWNS*...

...WAS *IMPOSSIBLE*. THERE *ARE* NO "*NEIGHBORING TOWNS*," MR. ARCHARD.

WHO SAYS THEY'VE GONE *ANYWHERE?*

I'VE BROUGHT A FEW *WITH* ME. THE *REST*?

AS I SAY, THEY CAN'T ENDURE *MUCH* TRAVEL... BUT IF IT'S A MATTER OF EXTERMINATING *PESTS*...

...WELL, THEY CAN *CERTAINLY* MAKE IT AS FAR AS A *GYPSY* ENCAMPMENT...

=HHGGKKK--!

EMMA!

IF YOU'VE *HURT* HER, I *SWEAR*--

--I'LL *NEVER* HEAR THE *END* OF IT!

*N*OT ANOTHER WORD IS *SPOKEN*.

WE'VE NO *TIME* FOR *REPARTEE*. WE HAVE TO WARN THE *GYPSIES* OF THE UPCOMING *ATTACK*.

GUIDED BY THE *WOMEN*, WE THUNDER TOWARDS THEIR CAMP AT *BREAKNECK SPEED*--

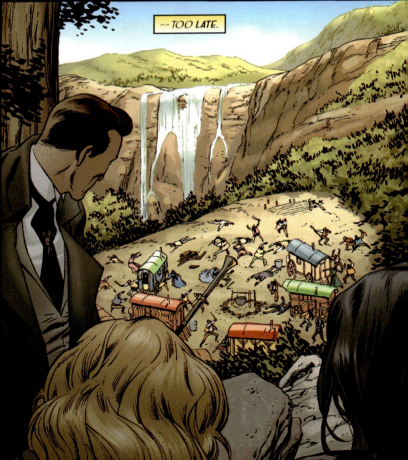

THE GYPSIES ARE UNDER FULL SIEGE--AND BY WHAT, THEY'VE NO IDEA.

DESPERATELY, THEY LOOK FOR SOMETHING TO HIT.

TELL THEM TO FOLLOW ME!

TO WHERE? HOW DO WE EVEN KNOW WE'RE RETREATING?

FASTER! WE'RE ALMOST THERE!

WHAT? SIMON, I CAN BARELY HEAR YOU! THE WATERFALL--!

EXACTLY.

NOW!

ATTACK!

BEAUTIFUL. IN ONE STROKE, THE TABLES ARE *TURNED*. THE VILLAGERS' ONLY REAL WEAPON WAS *SURPRISE*. TAKE THAT AWAY...

<YOU DARE COME AFTER US? WE MEANT YOU NO HARM→>

THEY'RE FLEEING! TO THE WAGONS AND AWAY WHILE THEY GATHER THEIR WOUNDED!

THERE'LL BE NO PURSUIT! ISN'T THAT RIGHT, BURGOMEISTER?

FOR NOW, MR. ARCHARD...FOR NOW. BUT THERE WILL BE RETRIBUTION... NO MATTER THAT IT TAKES A LIFETIME.

THE SUDDEN WINDWHISPER, THE GHOSTLY FOOTFALL... SOMEDAY, WHEN YOU LEAST EXPECT IT...

...THAT WILL BE US. THIS, I SWEAR.

WONDERFUL. HOW DO I NOT WORRY ABOUT *THAT* FOREVER?

BY CONTINUING TO CARRY A COSMETICS BAG WITH ITS OWN GRAVITATIONAL FIELD.

LET'S GO.

AS SIMON PREDICTED, WE DEPART WITHOUT INCIDENT.

AS A MEASURE OF GRATITUDE, THE GYPSIES OFFER US PASSAGE TO THE NEXT TOWN SO THAT WE MIGHT CATCH A TRAIN *HOME*.

...THREE PAIRS *SHOES*, TWO *BONNETS*, FOUR PAIRS *STOCKINGS*...

AN *EXPENSE VOUCHER* FOR ALL THE THINGS YOU MADE ME LEAVE *BEHIND*.

...ROUGE, POWDER, BLUSH, MASCARA IN *GREAT* VARIETY...WHAT ELSE...?

INFORMATION. MY NAME IS *SIMON ARCHARD*, AND--

YOU? YOU'RE--

HMMH.

WHAT?

I THOUGHT YOU'D BE *TALLER*, SOMEHOW.

SORRY TO *DISAPPOINT* YOU.

HARDLY ONE TO TALK, MYSELF.

SO LIGHTBOURNE *DID* SPEND TIME WITH YOU. HE *SPOKE* OF SIMON?

OH, AT STULTIFYING LENGTH. AND FREQUENTLY, BUT NEVER *KINDLY*, EVEN THOUGH HE OWES HIS *LIFE* TO YOU.

IN WHAT WAY?

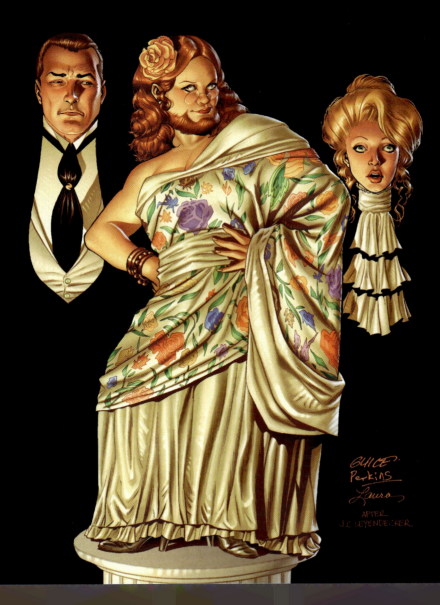

NOTHING.

ARRESTS F...
Extraordinary Scenes.

pursuing the brigands who Thurs-
...ved Eddowes Jewelry of the fa-
Sapphire, detectives Malcolm
...mon Archard exposed the

thieves as none...
...ins of proprietor Bli...
clues left by the daring...
...edly deduced and evaluated by the

...MT.
BOUTON
MURDER
SOLVED

Wednes...
Wynne B...
working in
District, was ap...
...y Malcolm Light
...d Simon Archar...
...l with the h...
...f Alice...

...EIGH...
GATE

...OMAN
...OCKINGLY
...OISONED!

...ng woman named Jane

...medicine. ...e she
...and ...some
...went o... ...e her
...sweets wi...young
...medicine. Trag...
...life was cut short by a dose of
...poison inside ...e sweets, an in-
...strument of murder which was
...intended for a Partington law-
...yer as part of an altogether sep-
...crime. The detection
...ncy of Lightbourne & Arch-
...d was the first to determine
...he truth behind Miss Beat-
...s untimely death, and
...in such matt...

Yet another additi...
to the long l...
avenged by the...
of Lightbourne...
Friday mornin...
ten o'clock, ju...
decked itself...
lands for the ...
a ...ting d...
a...

THE sensation of l...
has been Saturday's ...
by the Lightbourne-...
Agency, of the unique...
of killing employed in...
strom Murder. Foun...
in a room locked fro...
side with only a pud...
ter at his feet, Norman...
strom, it was presumed, c...
not have found purcha...
close to the ceiling wi...
some surface upon whi...
stand. However, no ch...
other object of th...

The horrible dens of vice and
crime that have so long
plagued our fair city have endured yet another upheaval at
the hands of Malcolm Lightbourne and Simon Archard.
Working with full governmen-
tal authority, th...
team t...

Great excitement was occasioned
this morning when it was reported
that detectives Malcolm Lightbourne and Simon Archard had
last exposed the secrets ...
the Mystery of the S...
Their investig...
light new...
Stath...

...RANGE
...CURENC...
...BL...MJIN...

PARTINGTON
GRATEFUL

...ollowing ...
...rouched for ...

...ng d... ...skeleton astrid...
...of a ro...ale green mare. Inquiries...
...bre...
...upon h...
...urne-A...
...y resid...

FOR WEEKS NOW, I'VE BEEN ATTEMPTING TO INVEIGLE FROM SIMON INFORMATION AS TO HIS PAST.

SPECIFICALLY, HIS PAST *PARTNER*--A MADMAN BY THE NAME OF *MALCOLM LIGHTBOURNE,* WHO WAS PRESUMED DEAD FOR MANY YEARS--

--A FALSE *ASSUMPTION* GIVEN THAT HE NEARLY *DROWNED* SIMON, SWUNG AT ME REPEATEDLY WITH AN *AXE,* AND IS CURRENTLY *AT LARGE.*

...SORTED, ONE WOULD HAVE TO ASSUME, BY *COLOR.*

THUS MY HUNT FOR ARTICLES REGARDING THE *LIGHTBOURNE-ARCHARD* TEAM IS *MADDENINGLY RANDOM...*

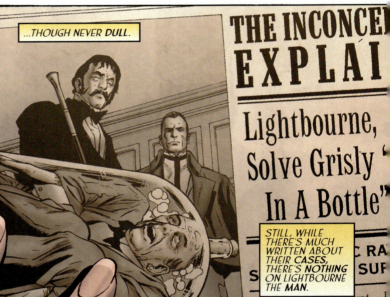

...THOUGH NEVER *DULL.*

THE INCONCE[I]
EXPLAI[N]

Lightbourne,
Solve Grisly

In A Bottle"

STILL, WHILE THERE'S MUCH WRITTEN ABOUT THEIR *CASES,* THERE'S *NOTHING* ON LIGHTBOURNE THE *MAN.*

PARTINGTON detectives yesterday found the body of numismatist Victor Q. Smythe, bizarrely encased in a corked

THANK YOU FOR YOUR ASSISTANCE ON THE HUMBERT MURDER.

SIMON! I DIDN'T HEAR YOU--

WAIT.

I WASN'T HELPING WITH THAT. I WAS HERE.

YOU DON'T *SAY.*

AH. HOW CONVENIENTLY WE IGNORE THAT YOU'VE BEEN SO ON THE MOVE THAT YOUR PARTNER--

ASSISTANT.

--*PARTNER* CAN'T FIND YOU, MUCH LESS *AID* YOU.

SPEAKING OF FINDING... THOSE ARE THE *MORGUE FILES,* YES?

OBITUARIES BY THE *HUNDRED.* DO YOU REALLY KEEP A RECORD OF EVERY SINGLE DEATH IN PARTINGTON?

A TOOL OF THE TRADE. AND WE CAN ADD A NEW *CLIPPING.*

AS USUAL, HOWEVER, SIMON IS ABOUT AS FORTHCOMING AS A *NUN* AT A *ROULETTE WHEEL.*

WHICH IS WHY I'VE BEEN IN *HERE* FOR THREE DAYS. SIMON OWNS PROBABLY THE SINGLE GREATEST LIBRARY COLLECTION IN THE WORLD, AND AMONG ITS REFERENCE WORKS ARE *DECADES'* WORTH OF BOUND NEWSPAPER VOLUMES...

Mmmh.

BONES ARE *CREAKING,* I'VE BEEN AT THIS SO LONG. AND STILL NO--

...

OH-HO. WHAT'S *THIS?*

OH.

ONE OF OUR *AGENTS* -- A STABLEBOY AT THE *OXFORD-COLLINS* STATE--JUST TELEPHONED WITH SOME VERY MUNDANE *REPORTAGE* REGARDING AN *UNFORTUNATE INCIDENT.*

JOIN ME.

BUT IF IT'S THAT *MUNDANE,* THEN WHY--

VERY WELL.

WHY, INDEED? WHY HAVE WE COMPLETELY ABANDONED THE HUNT FOR *LIGHTBOURNE?*

THE MANSION AND SURROUNDING ACREAGE BELONGING TO *LIONEL OXFORD-COLLINS* TOGETHER CONSTITUTE THE SINGLE LARGEST PRIVATELY-HELD AREA OF LAND IN PARTINGTON.

IT TAKES LONGER TO WALK AROUND THE SOUTH SIDE THAN IT DID TO HANSOM HERE FROM *SIMON'S* HEADQUARTERS.

QUITE THE *STROLL*. I WISH YOU'D WARNED ME TO PACK A *LUNCH*.

IT'S DIFFICULT TO DECIDE WHICH IS MORE MELLIFLUOUS TO THE EAR:

YOUR DRONING COMPLAINTS THAT I LEAVE YOU *BEHIND*, OR YOUR DRONING COMPLAINTS THAT I TAKE YOU *ALONG*.

YET I *DO* ADMIRE THE *SCENERY*.

...CONVEY MY *CONDOLENCES*, GIRLS. IF ONLY WE'D BEEN RIDING *WITH* HIM WHEN HE --

ARCHARD? WHAT ARE *YOU* DOING HERE?

WE'LL SEE.

AH. *GARFIELD BIGGS*. THE LAWYERLY *STENCH* GIVES HIM AWAY.

AN UNREPENTANT CHAUVINIST WHO CAN'T *ABIDE* SEEING A WOMAN UNCHAINED FROM HER *STOVE*. HE'S SOILED OUR PATH BEFORE.

WELL, YOU'RE NOT *WELCOME* HERE, GOOD SIR. THERE'S NO TAWDRY *CRIME* FOR YOU TO SCRUTINIZE, NO *BLOOD* IN WHICH TO BATHE YOUR *HANDS*.

THIS CAN'T BE *HAPPENING*. DOCTOR, *PLEASE*...!

...BUT HE'S *GONE*.

FOR A MOMENT, I THOUGHT HE COULD...

BUT NO. DAMNED TICKER JUST GAVE OUT.

I DID ALL I COULD FOR YOUR FATHER, GIRLS...

YOU'RE NOT ALONE. THE *CHURCH OF THE DRYADINE*-- NOTED WORSHIPPERS OF NATURE AND FAUNA-- MAKES ITS HOME ON THE GROUNDS IMMEDIATELY ADJACENT.

THEY'VE COUNTED OXFORD-COLLINS AS A MEMBER OF THEIR FAITH FOR *YEARS*...YEARS IN WHICH, I'M TOLD, THEY'VE BEEN TRYING TO COAX THEIR WAY INTO THE MAN'S *WILL*.

THAT'S AN ODD THING TO BRING *UP*, SIMON.

ODD...BUT *TIMELY*.

Oh, MY.

HEART ATTACK? WERE THERE ANY *WITNE*--

--I MEAN-- WAS THERE ANYONE WITH HIM AT THE TIME?

ALL OF *US*. EVERY FEW MONTHS, LIONEL ASSEMBLED HIS FRIENDS AND FAMILY AND UNLEASHED THE HOUNDS FOR A *GARGOYLE HUNT*.

THE BLAST OF LIONEL'S BUGLE SCATTERED US THROUGH THE WOODS IN TWOS AND THREES ON A MERRY CHASE.

"YOU'D BE SURPRISED AT HOW *STRENUOUS* RIDING CAN BE. JUST BECAUSE THE *HORSE* DOES MOST OF THE WORK DOESN'T MEAN YOUR MUSCLES WON'T *ACHE* AFTERWARDS.

"POOR LIONEL.

AS THE DOCTOR FINISHES HIS TALE, SOMEONE *NEW* SPEAKS, AND I CAN TELL JUST BY LOOKING AT HER THAT SHE'S A *POETIC SOUL.*

FAREWELL, KIND SIR. MAY GOD'S SOIL BLESS AND KEEP YOU.

AND MAY THE LEAVES AND THE FERNS AND THE FLOWERS LONG IN STEM WATCH AND PROTECT YOU AS THE SEASONS COME AND GO.

THE ILLS THAT FLESH IS HEIR TO...

AN *ANNOYINGLY* POETIC SOUL.

HOW *DARE* YOU LAY CLAIM TO WHAT'S *RIGHTFULLY OURS,* YOU FILTHY *HAG?*

THIS LAND IS TO BE SHARED WITH *BELIEVERS,* YOU INSOLENT *CHILD.*

IF YOU'RE GOING TO BICKER OVER *INHERITANCE,* CAN YOU AT LEAST GET THE POOR MAN INTO A *GRAVE* SO HE CAN *ROLL OVER* PROPERLY?

DE*LIGHT*FUL.

"THE EXERTION WAS TOO MUCH FOR HIM."

"BY THE TIME HE'D HIT THE GROUND, HE WAS ALREADY GREY AS THE *GRAVE*, EACH BREATH MORE SHALLOW THAN THE LAST."

"THOSE OF US CLOSEST TO HIM CARRIED HIM BACK TO THE HOUSE IMMEDIATELY... BUT *'IMMEDIATELY'* WASN'T FAST *ENOUGH*."

YRONDYNE. *HIGH PRIESTESS* OF THE DRYADINE SECT.

SHE DOESN'T EXACTLY REEK OF *SINCERITY*. AM I THE ONLY ONE WITH THAT IMPRESSION?

NO.

Oh, SAVE THE *CROCODILE TEARS*, YOU TREE-STROKING *FREAK*. THEY'RE A *WASTE*.

FATHER MAY HAVE BOUGHT INTO YOUR ARCANE CLAPTRAP. *WE*, ON THE OTHER HAND, WANT YOU AWAY FROM *HIM* AND OFF *OUR LAND*. NOW.

"YOUR" LAND. THE TINY *ACORNS* CLAIM TO KNOW HOW LEANED THE *OAK*. HOW *JOCUND*.

THAT *VOICE*.

WHEN *I* DIE, I HOPE *MY* MOURNING PERIOD LASTS MORE THAN *NINE SECONDS*.

I KNOW THAT VOICE. I...

WHAT? BUT *WHY?*

ISN'T IT *OBVIOUS?* BIGGS, YOU MUST HAVE A *COPY* OF THE WILL.

MAKE HER *PROVE* IT. AND DON'T LOOK AT *US.*

WE WERE ON THE *HUNT.*

AND YET, OFF ON YOUR *OWN.* I DON'T RECALL *SEEING* THE GIRLS THROUGHOUT MOST OF IT. OF COURSE, THEY COULD SAY THE SAME ABOUT *ME...*

SIMON, MY OFFICE HAS BEEN VANDALIZED AS WELL. LIONEL'S FILES ARE *GONE.*

YOU WERE HIS LAWYER. DO YOU KNOW THE SPECIFIC *DETAILS* OF HIS WILL?

AS PER LIONEL'S REQUEST, *NO.* HE WAS A *VERY* PRIVATE MAN.

I *CAN,* NEVERTHELESS, STATE WITH SOME CERTAINTY THAT THE ESTATE *EN TOTO* WAS LEFT *EITHER* TO THE DRYADINE CHURCH *OR* TO HIS DAUGHTERS BESS AND MARY, BUT *NOT* BOTH.

THIS LAND HAS BEEN IN LIONEL'S FAMILY FOR THREE CENTURIES. HE WAS ALWAYS ADAMANT THAT HE'D NEVER SPLIT IT UP.

BUT WHO *PROPERLY* INHERITS IT BECOMES A MATTER FOR *PROBATE COURT* SHOULD THE CHURCH CHALLENGE THE *GIRLS.*

AND WHY *SHOULDN'T* IT? DO YOU WANT TO KNOW HOW *DISAPPOINTED* LIONEL WAS IN THESE *ESURIENT* LITTLE *HARRIDANS* HE SIRED?

HOW *CONVINCED* HE WAS THAT THEY'D *SELL* THIS LAND TO SOULLESS DEVELOPERS WITHOUT A *MOMENT'S REGRET* SHOULD THEY BE ALLOWED THE *OPPORTUNITY?*

PLAINLY, *THEY* TURNED THIS OFFICE UPSIDE-DOWN!

WHY? WE *KNEW* WHERE THE *SAFE* WAS, UNLIKE *YOU,* YOU FATUOUS--

MR. ARCHARD, *ARREST* THIS WOMAN! SHE'S *GUILTY! GUILTY!* TAKE HER *AWAY!*

IN THE *FIRST* PLACE, THAT ISN'T WHAT I *DO.*

AND IN THE *SECOND* PLACE...

...I'M NOT INTERESTED IN *ANY* ACTIVITY THAT REQUIRES ENDURING ANOTHER *INSTANT* WITH *ANYONE* IN THAT ROOM.

YOU TOOK THE WORDS RIGHT OUT OF MY *MOUTH,* DARLING.

WRETCHED CREATURES, THE *LOT* OF THEM.

...SAID THE *POT* OF THE *KETTLE*...

CONTAINER HUMOR FROM THE *BOTTLE BLONDE.* COLOR ME *UNAMUSED.*

SEND HER *ALONG,* SIMON. THAT WAY, YOU AND I CAN PUT OUR...*HEADS* TOGETHER.

ABOUT THE MISSING *WILL?*

WELL, THERE'S THAT, *TOO.* I, IN FACT, HAVE A *THEORY* OR TWO...

ARE YOU *SURE?*

IT'S *NOT* OPHELIA.

ARE YOU *SURE?*

ARE YOU *SURE?*

IT'S *NOT* OPHELIA.

ARE YOU *SURE?*

IT'S *NOT* OPHELIA.

I DIDN'T KNOW THE CIRCUS WAS IN TOWN.

WE ROLLED THROUGH YESTERDAY. HELLO, SIMON.

EMMA, MEET *OPHELIA PRESSMONK,* OTTO'S *TWIN.*

TWIN *WHAT?*

AH. YOU MUST BE *EMMA BISHOP.*

EVERY TIME OTTO AND I VISITED THE *SNAKES* AT THE *ZOO,* HE MENTIONED *YOU.*

YES, DARLING, OUR MERRY CARAVAN ONCE MORE TRUNDLES INTO *PARTINGTON.*

VASHTI SENDS HIS BEST, BY THE WAY.

AND YOU'RE WITH US NOW *BECAUSE...?*

SAME REASON AS *YESTERDAY.* TO *BARGAIN.*

ON BEHALF OF THE *CIRCUS,* I APPROACHED MR. OXFORD-COLLINS ABOUT OUR SETTING UP ON THE NORTH-EAST CORNER OF HIS *ESTATE*--

--ONLY TO HAVE HIS *"LOVING"* DAUGHTERS *REBUFF* ME.

AND WE SHALL *AGAIN.*

IF YOU'VE THE *RIGHT.*

FIRST FLOOR, SOUTH WING. WE MET THERE FREQUENTLY. WHY?

YOU, YOU, AND YOU-- STAY WITH THE BODY UNTIL THE CORONER ARRIVES. THE REST OF YOU, FOLLOW *ME.*

TO *WHERE?*

SIMON?

SIMON?

AH, SIMON. SUCH A WAY WITH *PEOPLE* YOU HAVE...

IT OCCURS TO ME THAT, GIVEN ALL THE *SQUABBLING* ABOUT WHO INHERITS *WHAT*...

...AN EXAMINATION OF OXFORD-COLLINS' *LAST WILL AND TESTAMENT* MIGHT BE IN ORDER.

MR. BIGGS, CAN YOU VERIFY THAT THIS OFFICE IS WHERE HE WOULD HAVE KEPT SUCH AN IMPORTANT DOCUMENT?

YES.

THEN WE HAVE A *PROBLEM*.

EVIDENTLY, SOMEONE BEAT US *TO* IT.

ON FILE, YES.

SO WE *HOPE*.

TELEPHONE YOUR OFFICE IMMEDIATELY. ENQUIRE AS TO ITS SAFETY. TELL YOUR SECRETARY YOU WISH HER TO MAKE *CERTAIN* IT IS *IN HAND*.

WHAT A FINE TURN OF *EVENTS*. WHOEVER RANSACKED THE ROOM TURNED IT *UPSIDE-DOWN* IN SEARCH OF ITS SAFE.

WHO CAN ACCOUNT FOR THEIR WHERE-ABOUTS?

WHAT? IS ANYONE *HURT*?

MISS YRONDYNE, WHERE WERE YOU EARLIER THIS AFTER-NOON?

WHERE I AM EVERY DAY. ENGAGED IN PRIVATE *MEDITATION* AMIDST THE SYCAMORE GROVE NORTH OF THE *CHURCH*.

FINE. I'D ASK *HOW* YOU KNOW HER, BUT YOU WOULDN'T TELL ME. I'D ASK IF YOU YET KNOW WHO STOLE THE *WILL*, BUT YOU WON'T TELL ME THAT, *EITHER.*

SIMON, ALL REPARTEE ASIDE, YOU'RE GROWING *MORE* SECRETIVE AND *LESS* TRUSTING. IT'S *NOT* MY IMAGINATION. WHAT'S COME *BETWEEN* US?

...

ALL RIGHT. IT GOES BACK TO OUR ESCAPE FROM THAT SINKING *CARGO SHIP.*

DURING THE *MIRANDA CROSS* CASE.

WHEN WE RETURNED *HERE*, I FOUND A SINGLE STRAND OF LONG BLACK *HAIR* INSIDE MY COAT--

--UNTOUCHED BY THE *WATER.*

CURIOUS, I MOUNTED IT ON A MICROSCOPE SLIDE.

BLACK HAIR. *MIRANDA.* BUT I CAN'T TELL SIMON *SHE* WAS THERE WITHOUT SAYING TOO MUCH.

WHY WOULD YOU ASK ME?

BECAUSE, DURING MY ABSENCE *FOLLOWING* THAT CASE--

*T*HAT WENT POORLY.

I SHOULDN'T HAVE LET MY TEMPER GET THE BETTER OF ME. I SHOULD HAVE BEEN *KINDER* WITH SIMON...

...BECAUSE HE'S NOT *HIMSELF.* I'VE FINALLY GUESSED THE TRUTH ABOUT WHY HE'S AVOIDING THE MORE *PRESSING* CASE AT HAND.

IT'S *UNFATHOMABLE...* IT'S IN EVERY WAY *UNLIKE* SIMON...BUT IT'S THE ONLY THEORY THAT MAKES *SENSE.*

HE WAS YOUR FIRST *PARTNER*, SIMON, AND I SUSPECT HE WAS QUITE THE *MENTOR*, AS WELL.

THAT EXPLAINS THE *COMPETITIVE STREAK* HE STIRS IN YOU.

HE KNOWS HOW TO *GOAD* YOU, HOW TO *MANIPULATE* YOU.

YOU, OF *ALL* PEOPLE, MUST FIND THAT *TERRIFYING.*

BUT YOU HAVE TO PUT THAT FEAR *ASIDE*, SIMON, AND I'LL *HELP* YOU HOWEVER I *CAN.* I MEAN IT. YOU DON'T--

HERE.

--YOU DON'T *HAVE* TO BE *AFRAID* OF--

--AN ABSENCE IN WHICH YOU WERE THE ONLY PERSON WITH ACCESS *TO* THIS LAB--

--THE HAIR WAS *DESTROYED.*

IS THERE SOMETHING YOU WISH TO *TELL* ME?

FAR MORE THAN IS GOOD FOR YOU.

YOU'RE *ACCUSING* ME OF--?

SIMON ARCHARD, I HAVE *NO IDEA* WHAT BECAME OF YOUR *PRECIOUS EVIDENCE.* ON THAT, YOU HAVE MY *WORD.*

I'LL BE *DOWNSTAIRS* WHILE YOU DECIDE HOW YOU WISH TO *APOLOGIZE.*

COME TO ANY NEW OBSERVATIONS ABOUT *LIGHTBOURNE?*

YES.

YOU'RE *AFRAID* OF HIM.

I *SAW* HOW YOU REACTED WHEN THE GYPSIES SPOKE OF HIM, SIMON.

AND I *REMEMBER* HOW EMOTIONAL YOU BECAME BEFORE *THAT,* WHEN LIGHTBOURNE FIRST *ATTACKED.*

...

GOOD LORD.

IT'S I WHO MUST APOLOGIZE. THIS...

THEN YOU GRASP ITS SIGNIFICANCE.

I'M BEGINNING TO. WHY DIDN'T YOU BRING THIS UP BEFORE?

I HAD TO FIGURE OUT THE *WHY* OF IT FIRST. AND NOW THAT I *HAVE*--

"-- THE *'WHO'* OF IT IS PAINFULLY *APPARENT.*"

SO YOU SAY YOU KNOW WHO PINCHED LIONEL'S *WILL,* SIMON?

OF *COURSE* HE DOES! WHY *ELSE* ASSEMBLE THE *DRAMATIS PERSONAE* AT THE SCENE OF THE *CRIME?*

WHAT A FLAIR FOR *THEATRICS* YOU HAVE, MR. ARCHARD.

EXTRA POINTS FOR THE *THUNDERSTORM.*

THANK YOU. I FIND IT'S THOSE EXTRA *TOUCHES* THAT SET THE STAGE SO *BEAUTIFULLY* WHEN ONE DISCUSSES *MURDER.*

M-*MURDER?* BUT LIONEL WASN'T--

THAT'S *ABSURD!* DON'T KEEP US IN *SUSPENSE,* MAN! IF THE *THIEF* IS ALSO A *KILLER*--

PATIENCE, BIGGS. I REMIND YOU AGAIN, WHEN EMMA SPARKED DISCUSSION, NO ONE COULD PROVIDE HIMSELF A REASONABLE ALIBI FOR THE TIME OF THE THEFT.

THAT--

-- WAS *MY* JOB. NOTE THE *WINDOW PANE* CRACKED DURING THE BURGLARY.

WHEN EMMA AND I FIRST ARRIVED, WE CIRCUMNAVIGATED THE SOUTH WING--THIS WING. AT WHICH TIME THE WINDOWS WERE IN *PERFECT REPAIR.*

THE BROKEN GLASS SET THE THEFT *DURING THE PERIOD WE WERE ALL OUT BACK TOGETHER.*

WELL *OBSERVED,* MR. ARCHARD... AND *THANK* YOU. AT LEAST THAT CLEARS US.

OF *WHAT?*

EXCUSE ME...?

HE MOST CERTAINLY *WAS*. *THIS*, I'VE KNOWN FROM THE *START*. AND HIS *HUNTSMAN'S BUGLE* WAS THE *WEAPON*.

A QUICK SWAB OF ITS MOUTHPIECE EVINCED A SLOW-ACTING NICOTINE-DERIVATIVE *POISON*--

--ITS EFFECTS INDISTINGUISHABLE FROM A COMMON *CORONARY*.

HOW PERFECTLY *GHASTLY!* WHO WOULD HAVE..?

ANY OF YOU, FRANKLY. I'M QUITE CONFIDENT THE BUGLE WASN'T HARD TO *GET* AT. MOREOVER, NO ONE OFFERS A CLEAR ALIBI FOR *ANYTHING*, AND WITH THE *INHERITANCE* AT STAKE, MOTIVES *ABOUND*... INCLUDING *YOURS*, BIGGS.

MINE? YOU'RE *MAD!* WHAT *POSSIBLE* REASON COULD I HAVE FOR MURDERING LIONEL?

YOU SAID IT *YOURSELF*. WITH THE WILL *MISSING*, THE OXFORD-COLLINS *DAUGHTERS* COULD SPEND *YEARS...EXPENSIVE* YEARS...IN COURT AS YOU DEFEND THEIR *CLAIM*.

I NEVER SAID THE MURDERER AND THE THIEF WERE ONE AND THE SAME. *BIGGS* DID. AND WE *ALL* KNOW HOW OFTEN A *LAWYER* SPEAKS THE TRUTH.

THE IDENTITY OF THE *KILLER* IS NO MYSTERY AT *ALL*. AS A MATTER OF *FACT*, I KNEW *PRECISELY* WHO WAS GUILTY THE MOMENT I WAS *NOTIFIED* OF OXFORD-COLLINS' *FATE*... BEFORE I EVEN LEFT MY *HEADQUARTERS*.

THE PENNY ARCA...

Afternoon Edition, Price Ha'...

ly Illustrated

MacGRUDER KILLER FOU...

VICTIM'S CHILDREN WERE MASTERMINDS

INSTRUMENT OF HIS DEATH

MEMORIES ARE *SHORT*. WHILE *SOMEONE* WOULD EVENTUALLY HAVE MADE THE CONNECTION, I RECALLED IT *INSTANTLY*... AS WAS THE MACABRE *INTENT* OF THE CRIME'S SECRET *ENGINEER*.

TWELVE YEARS AGO, PARTINGTON SAW A MURDER ALMOST *IDENTICAL*--RIGHT DOWN TO THE *VERY LAST DETAIL*.

I REMEMBER THIS *VIVIDLY*--

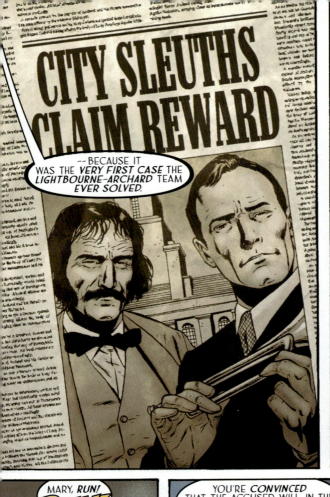

CITY SLEUTHS CLAIM REWARD

--BECAUSE IT WAS THE *VERY FIRST CASE* THE *LIGHTBOURNE-ARCHARD* TEAM EVER SOLVED.

HE NEVER *TOLD* YOU THAT YOU WERE PAWNS IN A *LARGER SCHEME*, DID HE, GIRLS?

WE...WE DON'T KNOW WHAT YOU'RE *TALKING* ABOUT...!

MARY, *RUN!* **RUN!**

I'VE BEEN *MEANING* TO SPEAK TO YOU ABOUT THIS. DESPITE YOUR *MANY* BRILLIANT TALENTS, YOU *DO* HAVE *ONE* GLARING FLAW.

YOU'RE *CONVINCED* THAT THE ACCUSED WILL, IN THE FACE OF YOUR *GENIUS*, FALL AND *PROSTRATE* THEMSELVES AND BEG *FORGIVENESS*.

YOU *MIGHT* WISH TO TAKE INTO ACCOUNT THAT, MORE OFTEN, THEY *FLEE.*

NOW WHO HAS ISSUES OF TRUST?

OPHELIA, TAKE THE *KEY* AND *MEET* US. THE MATTER OF WHICH WE SPOKE *BEFOREHAND?*

ATTENDED TO...

SPARE ME.

LIGHTBOURNE'S BEHIND IT *ALL*. HE SOUGHT YOU *OUT*-- A CHARMING *STRANGER* WITH A *PLAN*, AWARE OF YOUR *GREED*.

HE *PROPOSED* THE MURDER AND INSTRUCTED YOU IN THE *MECHANICS*.

AFTERWARD, WHILE WE WERE GATHERED, *HE* STOLE THE *WILL*--

--PILLAGING THE ROOM, NO DOUBT, TO COVER THE FACT THAT YOU'D *TOLD* HIM EXACTLY WHERE IT *WAS*.

TOGETHER, YOU--

WHUNF

≈KAFF≈

"...AS THEY'LL SOON *LEARN*."

QUICKLY! TO THE *STABLES*! WE CAN MAKE OUR ESCAPE BY *HORSEBACK*!

"Oh, TO *BE* THERE."

BESS, THE *DOORS*--!

I *SEE*! SHUT *UP* AND LET ME *THINK*!

≈GASP≈

NO! BESS, HE'S *COMING!* HE KNOWS WHERE WE *ARE!*

WERE. HE KNOWS WHERE WE *WERE.*

THIS WAY!

GOD, I CAN BARELY *SEE...*

I CAN SEE *ENOUGH!* UP *THERE!*

POLICE CLOSING IN. *DAMN* YOU, ARCHARD.

BESS, WHAT'LL WE *DO?* LIGHTBOURNE WILL *KILL* US IF WE'RE CAUGHT! *HE'LL KILL US!*

SHUT UP! GET TO THE *LAKE!*

WELL *PLAYED.*

CHESS WITH *HALFWITS.*

SO LIGHTBOURNE SET THIS WHOLE AFFAIR IN MOTION SIMPLY TO *TAUNT* YOU?

NO.

THERE'S MORE TO THIS, LADIES! *WHAT'S LIGHTBOURNE HIDING ON THE ESTATE?*

TELL ME!

WE'LL →SPPT SPUTT← WE'LL *NEVER--*

YOU SHUT UP, BESS! IT'S *OVER!*

AS--AS PART OF OUR *DEAL,* HE TOLD US TO KEEP THE *CIRCUS* PEOPLE AWAY AT *ALL COSTS*-- BUT HE WOULDN'T SAY *WHY!*

HE PROMISED IF WE PLAYED *ALONG,* WE'D GET THE INHERITANCE *PLUS* PAYMENT FROM *HIM!* AND THAT'S *ALL WE KNOW*-- I *SWEAR!*

PROBABLY *SO.* IF ANYTHING *ELSE* COMES TO MIND, TELL IT TO THE *POLICE.*

"WHAT'S LIGHTBOURNE *HIDING?"* WHAT DO YOU MEAN BY *THAT?*

IT'S *OBVIOUS...*

...THOUGH I ADMIT OPHELIA'S *PRESENC* MADE IT *CLEARER* TO ME.

I'D BEEN PROFOUNDLY MISTAKEN.

SIMON HADN'T BEEN IGNORING LIGHTBOURNE AT ALL. FAR FROM IT.

IT'S BEEN ABOUT LIGHTBOURNE ALL ALONG.

SIMON KNEW FROM THE START THAT THE TWO OF THEM WERE ENMESHED IN A MORBID AND JEOPARDOUS GAME...

...AND THAT LIGHTBOURNE DETERMINED THE PLAYING FIELD.

HELLO SIMON!

IT'S *OVER*, MALCOLM...*STEM* THE FLOW OF THIS UNDERGROUND RIVER AND I'LL SHOW YOU LENIENCY.

LURING ME INTO YOUR TRAP ONLY HASTENED *ENDGAME*.

BUT NOW...YOUR QUAINT LITTLE CITY IS *HEMORRHAGING!*

HA!

SIMON ARCHARD MAY BE ARROGANT AND BOORISH AND UNABASHEDLY *RUDE*...

...BUT LIGHTBOURNE IS DIABOLICAL AND CRUEL AND UNREPENTANTLY *EVIL*.

AND I WOULD KICK HIM *MYSELF* IF I HAD MORE SOLID FOOTING.

I SEE YOU'VE DEVELOPED A SENSE OF *HUMOR* DURING MY LONG ABSENCE.

PARTINGTON WAS MERELY *BLEEDING* FROM MY FIRST INCISION, SIMON.

KCHAK

SIMON, IT'S ALL COMING APART DOWN HERE!

I'M *UNDERSTATING*, OF COURSE.

LIGHTBOURNE'S WATERWORKS MOST CERTAINLY LIVES UP TO HIS EXPECTATIONS.

WE ARE VERY LIKELY DOOMED.

YOU JUST HAVEN'T ACCEPTED IT YET.

EMMA!

WATER-LOGGED *AGAIN*, I SEE.

CONSIDER THIS AN OBJECT LESSON IN THE VALUE OF CHOOSING *DISCRETION* OVER VALOR.

SIMON...?

WHAT...WHAT WAS *THAT* ABOUT?

YOU...ahem...YOU HAD DROWNED, MISS BISHOP.

I WAS MERELY...uh... BREATHING *LIFE* BACK INTO YOUR LUNGS.

YOUR *UNORTHODOX* STUDY HABITS, NO DOUBT.

...OR PERHAPS YOU'VE BEEN *DABBLING* IN *BLACK RITES?*

OH, NO...*NO,* MR. LIGHTBOURNE.

IT'S MERELY A *SCIENTIFIC* EXPLORATION.

I'VE *POSTULATED* THAT ONE CAN *FIX* THE TIME OF DEATH...

...BY EXAMINATION OF THE CONTENTS PRESENT IN THE DECEDENT'S GASTRIC PATH.

I *DID* AID THE POLICE IN A MURDER MYSTERY VERY RECENTLY.

DO TELL.

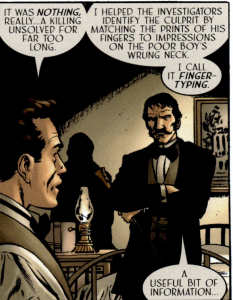

IT WAS *NOTHING,* REALLY...A KILLING UNSOLVED FOR FAR TOO LONG.

I HELPED THE INVESTIGATORS IDENTIFY THE CULPRIT BY MATCHING THE PRINTS OF HIS FINGERS TO IMPRESSIONS ON THE POOR BOY'S WRUNG NECK.

I CALL IT *FINGER-TYPING.*

A USEFUL BIT OF INFORMATION...

...PERHAPS AS IMPORTANT AS THE VICTIM'S OWN NAME.

MICHAEL LIGHTBOURNE.

QUITE SO. YOU'VE DEMONSTRATED MORE FORWARD-THINKING IN YOUR *AMATEUR* INVESTIGATIONS THAN PARTINGTON'S FINEST HAVE SHOWN IN THRICE THAT TIME.

BUT, SIR... I'M NOT THE MOST *CONVERSATIONAL* SORT.

I'VE NEVER HAD MANY FRIENDS. NOT IN THE ORPHAN HOUSE, NOT HERE...

AND YOU'RE THE *BETTER* FOR IT.

TRUST ME, SIMON...

...FRIENDSHIP AND LOYALTY WILL BE NOTHING MORE THAN IMPEDIMENTS TO YOUR *GREATER* CALLING...

302

ARCHARD

BARTLESB

SOMERS, R.

O'HERLIHY, D.

THANKFULLY, A DRAMATIC *PAUSE*. HAVING SURVIVED MALCOLM LIGHTBOURNE'S WATERWORKS ENGINEERED TO SWALLOW UP PARTINGTON, SIMON AND I FIND OURSELVES SUBJECTED TO A VERY *DIFFERENT* TORTURE.

LIGHTBOURNE IS TRAPPED AMONG THE SODDEN WRECKAGE, YET WIELDS A DRY AND DEADLY FIREARM...AND AWFUL TRUTHS LONG *UNREVEALED*.

DID YOU *REALLY* MEET HIM THIS WAY, SIMON?

OF COURSE HE *DID*, MISS BISHOP!

IT WAS LIKELY THE BEST DAY OF *BOTH* OUR LIVES, eh, SIMON?

"IN JUST FIVE YEARS, OUR RENOWN HAD GROWN CONSIDERABLY... AS HAD OUR *CLIENTELE*."

"THE EPIPHANIC CHURCH RARELY EMPLOYED OUTSIDERS IN THEIR AFFAIRS.

"OUR INVOLVEMENT WAS *TESTAMENT* TO THE FAR-REACHING REPUTATION OF LIGHTBOURNE AND ARCHARD..."

...WHOSE INVESTIGATORY SKILLS ARE *UNSURPASSED*, I HEAR TELL.

PERHAPS THEN YOU MIGHT SEE FIT TO TRAIN YOUR DEDUCTIVE *LIGHT* UPON A CASE OF STOLEN PROPERTY.

AN ARTIFACT ONLY RECENTLY UNEARTHED AND OF GREAT...*CONCERN*... TO THE CHURCH HAS GONE MISSING, ABSCONDED FROM OUR CARE.

THERE WAS NO BETTER PUPIL... SO EAGER TO *LEARN,* SO EAGER TO *PLEASE* HIS MENTOR...

HE...HE... ehn...MY LEG IS *SHATTERED...* RENT IN TWO.

I CAN SEE *BONE...* AND I SEEM TO BE LOSING QUITE A LOT OF BLOOD.

IF NOT FOR *SHOCK,* I VENTURE I WOULD NOT BE SO LUCID ABOUT...ihn... *THE PAST.*

SHALL I... I ihn...SHALL I *CONTINUE?*

YOUR WORSHIP, PERHAPS IF YOU COULD BE MORE *SPECIFIC* ABOUT THIS ITEM--

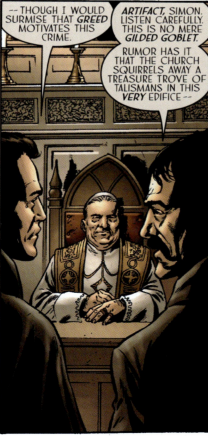

--THOUGH I WOULD SURMISE THAT *GREED* MOTIVATES THIS CRIME.

ARTIFACT, SIMON. LISTEN CAREFULLY. THIS IS NO MERE *GILDED GOBLET.* RUMOR HAS IT THAT THE CHURCH SQUIRRELS AWAY A TREASURE TROVE OF TALISMANS IN THIS *VERY* EDIFICE--

--*SORCEROUS* ARTIFACTS KEPT UNDER LOCK AND LATCH TO GUARD US LESS *ENLIGHTENED* FROM THEIR SINISTER INFLUENCE.

AM I NOT *CORRECT,* YOUR WORSHIP?

MAGIC IS NOTHING BUT *POPPYCOCK.*

IF ONLY THAT WERE *TRUE,* MR. ARCHARD...

BUT THIS POPPYCOCK HAS A *NAME*.

ACCORDING TO SCRIPTURE IT IS A JEWEL OF NEFARIOUS POWER.

AND IN OUR TONGUE IT IS KNOWN IN CERTAIN INFAMY AS THE *ENIGMATIC PRISM*.

SOME SORT OF SORCEROR'S STONE? SURELY YOU ARE *JESTING*, FATHER...

THE ENIGMATIC PRISM...

"CLEARLY YOU ARE *INFORMED* ON PENBERTHY'S TRAVELS, MR. LIGHTBOURNE.

"THE CHURCH, EXPECTING HIS ARRIVAL, DISPATCHED TWO EMISSARIES THIS MORN TO ACCOMPANY THE PRISM TO MY CHARGE.

"THEY WERE LATER FOUND DEAD, PENBERTHY HIMSELF GONE *MISSING*.

"THE JEWEL'S *CURSE* HAS LIKELY STRUCK ONCE MORE.

"NO ONE KNOWS ITS ORIGINS, THOUGH THE PRISM IS BELIEVED TO BE MANY CENTURIES OLD...ITS VALUE *INCALCULABLE*.

"AS SUCH, IT HAS RARELY PASSED HANDS THROUGH *BENIGN* CIRCUMSTANCE.

"THERE ARE WHISPERS THAT THE JEWEL IS *ALLURING*...

"TO GAZE INTO ITS RADIANT FIRE IS TO LOSE SIGHT OF *ALL* REASON AND DESIRE NOTHING BUT THE *PRISM ITSELF*...

"...TO SURRENDER TO ONE'S *BASEST* DESIRES."

I HAD THOUGHT IT ONLY *LEGEND*.

SIMON, IF IT INDEED *EXISTS*--

OH, THE PRISM IS MORE THAN *STORIED*, MR. LIGHTBOURNE.

THE *EPIPHANIC CHURCH* HAD CONTRACTED THE FAMED ARCHAEOLOGIST *PENBERTHY* TO SEEK OUT AND PROCURE THE JEWEL FOR OUR...*STUDY*.

CLIVE PENBERTHY, THE ADVENTURER WHOSE SHIP WAS INBOUND FOR *PARTINGTON* THIS VERY MORNING?

A TRICK OF THE LIGHT, YOUR EMINENCE.

LIGHT REFRACTED IN SUCH A WAY TO RESEMBLE FLAMES.

AND IN OUR EXPERIENCE, *AVARICE* *ALWAYS* BRINGS OUT THE WORST IN MAN--

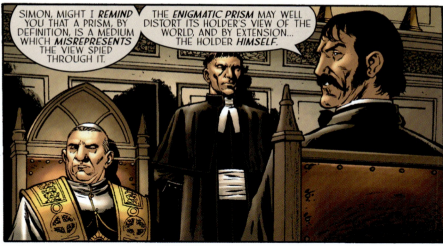

SIMON, MIGHT I *REMIND* YOU THAT A PRISM, BY DEFINITION, IS A MEDIUM WHICH *MISREPRESENTS* THE VIEW SPIED THROUGH IT.

THE *ENIGMATIC PRISM* MAY WELL DISTORT ITS HOLDER'S VIEW OF THE WORLD, AND BY EXTENSION... THE HOLDER *HIMSELF*.

REST EASY, CARDINAL INVICTUS...

PENBERTHY AND THE JEWEL CAN'T BE *FAR*.

THERE ARE ONLY *SO* MANY PLACES ONE CAN TRAFFIC IN STOLEN GEMS...

SURELY, PARTINGTON'S MOST *LOQUACIOUS* INFORMANT MUST HAVE *SOMETHING* TO SAY ON THIS MATTER?

MORE MONEY TO PASS ALONG TO PENNY? CREDITORS BARKIN' DOWN HIS DOOR?

JUST PLAY ALONG AND FEIGN A BIT OF FRIGHT...

Uh... RIGHT.

...DON'T HIT ME!

STRIKE YOU, COLQUIN?

WHATEVER GAVE YOU SUCH A THOUGHT?

WELL, THE WAY YOU'RE LEVELING THAT WALKING STICK LIKE IT'S A PIKE FOR A PIG...

MERELY EMBELLISHING MY *POINT*, COLQUIN.

CONTINUE.

...THERE'S... uh...THERE'S LOTS OF SCUTTLEBUTT CIRCULATING ABOUT ON PENNY...uh... *PENBERTHY.*

GO ON.

I'D EVEN WAGER T'SAY THAT ME AN' ROLLY ARE WILLIN' T'GO *FARTHER* FOR BOTH OF 'EM.

RIGHT, ROLLY?

RIGHT, NASH.

SO, IF YOU THINK THAT PONCY *CANE* IS A MATCH FOR ROLLY'S *BLADE* OR MY *SAP* --

KLOP

YOU WERE *SAYING*, MISTER NASH?

BRAVO, SIMON. WE WERE LIKELY OUTMATCHED IN BRAWN, YET YOU MEASURED THE SITUATION AND APTLY USED THE FIELD OF BATTLE TO OUR *ADVANTAGE*.

I THOUGHT IT BEST TO HASTEN OUR EXIT AND CONTINUE THE HUNT. WHERE NOW?

PERHAPS WE SHOULD COMMENCE TO WHERE *ALL* OF MISTER PENBERTHY'S TREASURES GO...

"PARTINGTON'S ARCHIVE OF ANTIQUITIES.

"WHERE *ELSE* WOULD ONE EXPECT TO FIND A TREASURE-HUNTER AND HIS *ILL-GOTTEN BOOTY?*"

YOUR HELP IS MUCH *APPRECIATED*, DOCTOR SMITHEE.

OF ALL THE ITEMS I CURATE, THIS I'M AFRAID IS *ALL* WE HAVE IN THE COLLECTION WHICH MAKES MENTION OF THE *ENIGMATIC PRISM*.

SKASH

...AND I WILL PROCEED TO *DE-CLAW* MISTER PENBERTHY.

NOT BLOODY LIKELY!

THE CLAWS OF SEPTA ARE *KEEN* BLADES...

I DUG THEM UP WHILE FENDING OFF CANNIBAL SAVAGES.

ROUTING *YOU* WILL BE AS EASY!

AHH!

HEED MY WORDS, SIMON.

DO NOT LET IT HAPPEN *EVER* AGAIN.

PENBERTHY WON'T GET FAR.

THE ECOND EVEL...!

A PRECISION EAR AS ALWAYS, SIMON...

I *FOUND* YOU AND I'LL *KEEP* YOU...

CLAWS OF SEPTA
COURTESY OF
PENBERTHY EXPEDITION

MISTER PENBERTHY, I PRESUME?

WHAT DO YOU WANT WITH ME?!

BAR THE DOOR, SIMON...

KRASH

MALCOLM, YOU'RE STABBED!

I'M FINE! THE QUARRY, SIMON! *THE QUARRY!*

PENBERTHY CAN *WAIT*, MALCOLM. YOUR WOUND CANNOT.

WHAT HAVE I TOLD YOU?! PENBERTHY HAS ESCAPED BECAUSE YOU ALLOWED *EMOTION* TO GET IN THE WAY OF BETTER JUDGMENT!

I SUSPECT I KNOW WHERE HE'LL APPEAR NEXT.

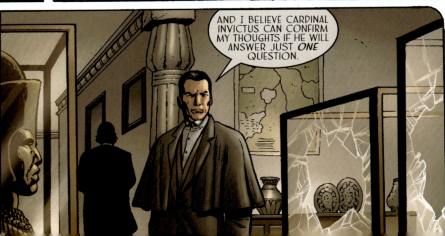

AND I BELIEVE CARDINAL INVICTUS CAN CONFIRM MY THOUGHTS IF HE WILL ANSWER JUST *ONE* QUESTION.

WELL, *THAT* CERTAINLY EXPLAINS A GREAT DEAL.

DON'T JUDGE HIM TOO *HARSHLY,* MISS BISHOP.

SIMON ARCHARD MAY BE A COLD FISH BY MY OWN *ENCOURAGEMENT...*

BUT FOR WHAT HE LACKS IN *EMPATHY,* SIMON MAKES UP IN INTELLIGENCE AND REASONING SKILL BEYOND THE AVERAGE.

HE'S A *SMART* ONE, OUR BOY... ALBEIT AMBIVALENT TO A FAULT.

HE *DOES* ME *PROUD.*

"I ASSURE YOU THAT *THIS* WAS NOT THE CASE ALL THOSE YEARS AGO, ESPECIALLY AFTER HE HAD DEFEATED HIS STAMMER.

"INTERESTINGLY, AS WE HURRIED AFTER PENBERTHY... SIMON POINTED OUT THE IRONY THAT OUR QUEST FOR THE ENIGMATIC PRISM WOULD BOTH *BEGIN* AND *END* AT THE EPIPHANIC CHURCH.

"ACTUALLY, THAT'S NOT QUITE TRUE.

"IT WOULD END IN THE CHURCH'S INFAMOUS *MUSEUM OBSCURA.*

SIMON, CAN ALL THIS BE *TRUE?*

I HAD ASSUMED THAT YOU WERE BIRTHED...FULLY... FORMED...

YOU... YOU'RE NOT *LISTENING.*

*A*ND WHY *SHOULD* HE?

ALTHOUGH LIGHTBOURNE IS AMUSED BY THIS PROMENADE DOWN MEMORY LANE, SIMON DOESN'T SHARE HIS MERRIMENT.

NONE OF THIS IS LAUGHABLE TO SIMON...AND THE REASONS NO DOUBT ARE ABOUT TO BE FULLY ILLUMINATED.

QUITE UNCHARACTERISTIC OF HIM TO BE SO *LACONIC,* MISS BISHOP.

KRITCH KRITCH

"PENBERTHY HAD BEEN THERE *BEFORE,* OF COURSE. HIS EMINENCE *CONFIRMED* THAT TO SIMON'S INQUIRY.

"PENBERTHY'S BALLYHOOED EXPEDITIONS HAD, IN FACT, *STOCKED* THIS SECRET CACHE OF ARCANE ARTIFACTS.

"HE KNEW THIS PLACE ALL TOO WELL."

"IMAGINE HIS SURPRISE THEN WHEN HE EYED THE ENIGMATIC PRISM HIDING IN *PLAIN SIGHT.*"

BUT... BUT...

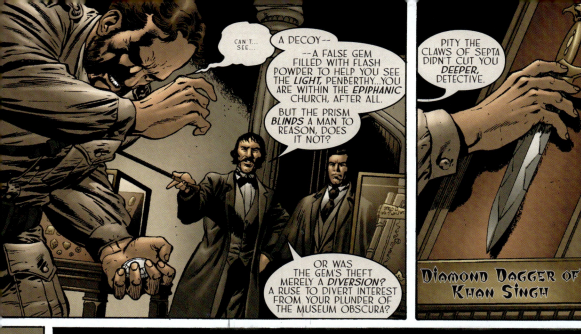

CAN'T... SEE...

A DECOY-- --A FALSE GEM FILLED WITH FLASH POWDER TO HELP YOU SEE THE *LIGHT,* PENBERTHY...YOU ARE WITHIN THE *EPIPHANIC* CHURCH, AFTER ALL.

BUT THE PRISM *BLINDS* A MAN TO REASON, DOES IT NOT?

OR WAS THE GEM'S THEFT MERELY A *DIVERSION?* A RUSE TO DIVERT INTEREST FROM YOUR PLUNDER OF THE MUSEUM OBSCURA?

PITY THE CLAWS OF SEPTA DIDN'T CUT YOU *DEEPER,* DETECTIVE.

DIAMOND DAGGER OF KHAN SINGH

THE PRISM IS INDEED A BEAUTIFUL BAUBLE, CLIVE.

SO TEMPTING...SO *IRRESISTIBLE.*

IS IT REALLY *WORTH* ALL THE EFFORT?

IT'S MINE!

YOU SAID IT YOURSELF, MISTER PENBERTHY...

I FOUND IT, I SHALL *KEEP* IT.

BUT I *KILLED* FOR IT!

I... I...

SKUCH

YOU DON'T *DESERVE* IT, CLIVE.

YOU *KILLED* HIM.

LEST HE KILL *YOU*, SIMON. I SAVED YOUR UNGRATEFUL LIFE AND I DID IT WITH AN EMOTIONAL DETACHMENT YOU HAVE *YET* TO LEARN.

I KNOW NOW THAT THE LEGENDS ARE *FALSE*.

THE PRISM DOES NOT DISTORT ONE'S WORLDVIEW... IT *CLARIFIES* IT.

I *ALONE* SHOULD POSSESS IT.

CAN YOU SEE THE FLICKER OF BLUE FIRE AT ITS CENTER?

A TRICK OF THE LIGHT, SIMON?

DOES IT DANCE FOR YOU ALSO?

SIMON, THE *FIRE*.

WE HAVEN'T MUCH TIME. LET'S DISCUSS THIS LATER LIKE OLD *FRIENDS*.

NO, MALCOLM. WE DISCUSS IT *NOW*.

I IMAGINE YOU CONVINCED PENBERTHY THAT *YOU* COULD EASE HIS MONEY WOES BY ENGINEERING A CRIME THAT PARTINGTON'S GREATEST DETECTIVE *COULDN'T* SOLVE.

DO YOU WISH ME TO ADMIT IT ALL?

IS THAT THE AFFIRMATION YOU DESIRE?

WOULD THAT MAKE YOU FEEL BETTER... *SMARTER*... THAN ME, SIMON?

VERY WELL, THEN... *HAVE* YOUR CONFESSION --

I DID IT.

I TOLD PENBERTHY THAT HE'D BEEN BETRAYED, HIMSELF *ROBBED* OF A LIFETIME OF SERVICE.

I'VE NO WISH TO *HURT* YOU!

SPARE ME YOUR *LIES*, MALCOLM!

I'VE ⇒UHN⇐ HEARD QUITE ENOUGH OF THEM TODAY.

"IN THE END, EVERYTHING YOU BELIEVED ALL CAME TUMBLING DOWN, SIMON."

THIS INFERNAL PLACE IS A *TINDERBOX!* WE SHOULD DISCUSS YOUR GUILT IN LESS *TENTATIVE* ENVIRONS, MY--

I THINK I'D MUCH RATHER END *HERE*... BE BURNED UP WITH ALL OF THESE *EVIL OLD RELICS.*

MALCOLM....

...DESPITE YOUR *DUPLICITY*, I DON'T WISH TO SEE MY...*MENTOR*... PERISH THIS WAY.

I SAID *NO.* I WON'T FACE PUBLIC HUMILIATION AS PARTINGTON PARADES ME TO THE *GALLOWS.*

BUT YOU ONLY CAME BACK FOR THE PRISM.

ACTUALLY...

I CAME BACK FOR *BOTH*.

AND IF I CAN'T HAVE *ONE*...

...I'LL HAVE THE OTHER!

DOWN, EMMA!

NO, SIMON... NOT--

BLAM BLAM

--buh... THE WATER.

LIGHTBOURNE?

GONE. HE FIRED HIS TWO SHOTS.

GIVEN THE STATE OF HIS SUBTERRANEAN LAIR, HE'S LIKELY GONE *ABOVE* GROUND NOW.

WE NEED TO FIND HIS BOLTHOLE TO THE SURFACE.

IMMEDIATELY.

YES, OF COURSE... JUST ALLOW ME A MOMENT TO CATCH MY BREATH.

WE HAVEN'T THE TIME, EMMA.

WE'VE GOT TO FIND MALCOLM *NOW*--

--BEFORE HE REALIZES HE ALREADY *HAS* THE ENIGMATIC PRISM!

HAD WE TRULY SEEN THE LIGHT, BOTH SIMON AND I WOULD HAVE REALIZED THAT SURVIVING LIGHTBOURNE ONCE WAS *HAPPENSTANCE*.

TWICE COULD LIKELY BE MERE *COINCIDENCE*.

A THIRD TIME WOULD SURELY CALL FOR NO LESS THAN DIVINE *PROVIDENCE*.

FIRE AND RUMBLING AND DARK CREATURES ON THE WING.

ONE CAN SCARCELY DISCERN THE CRIES OF THE *WOUNDED* FROM THE SHRIEKS OF THE *GARGOYLES* LITTERING THE SKY.

THE CREATURES ARE IN A...*FEEDING* FRENZY.

SIMON, THAT MAN...

DEAD. FRIGHTENED TO DEATH BY THE LOOKS OF IT.

AND THE GARGOYLES... THEY'RE *NOT*--

SKREEEEK!

I CAN ONLY *HOPE.*

BUT I FEAR IT'S MERELY *WISHFUL* THINKING THAT THEIR APPETITES ARE BEING *SATED* BY THE TIDE OF RATS WHICH LED US HERE.

NONE OF THIS IS *YOUR* FAULT, SIMON.

LIGHTBOURNE IS BEYOND REASON *OR* RATIONAL THOUGHT.

AND I AM THE *FOCUS* OF THAT MADNESS.

NO ONE NEAR ME IS *SAFE.*

LADYBIRD *NELL?*

WHAT'S THE MATTER, NELL? ARE YOU *HURT?*

NOT ME, LASS...*THE GIRLS!*

THE HOUSE HAS FALLEN AND NO ONE WILL HELP ME!

SIMON!

*T*HERE'S NO STOPPING HIM.

THIS ROW WITH LIGHTBOURNE WILL LIKELY END WITH ONE OR BOTH OF THEM ON THE SLAB.

NELL, HOW *BAD* IS IT?

HOW FAR DOES THE DAMAGE *EXTEND?*

MOST ALL OF TAMMANY AND DOWNTOWN ARE POCKED AND PITTED BY THESE SINKY *CRATERS*...

I KNEW HER. NOT WELL...

...BUT ENOUGH TO KNOW THAT SHE *DIDN'T* DESERVE TO BE A CASUALTY OF THIS ESCALATING CONFLICT WITH LIGHTBOURNE.

I 'MEMBER WHEN SHE DRESSED YOU UP IN THAT PRETTY RED DRESS.

YOU LOOKED SO LOVELY.

YOU DID TOO, PETE.

SHE'S BREATHING, PETE...JUST *BARELY*, THOUGH.

KRFRERKK

BEST DO IT *QUICK*, MIZ EMMA... ROOF'S »UHRN« GONNA COME CRASHIN' IN...

I SHOULD HAVE *KNOWN* PETE WOULD INSIST ON *ACCOMPANYING* ME.

WHOLE *CITY'S* FALLIN' TA *PIECES,* MIZ EMMA.

WHAT'S THIS *ABOUT?*

SOMEONE GOT A *BEEF* WITH MISTER ARCHARD?

YOU COULD SAY THAT, PETE...

YOU MIGHT REMEMBER THE EMINENT MALCOLM LIGHTBOURNE.

MISTER ARCHARD'S OLD *DETECTIN'* PARTNER? THE ROGUE WHO WENT MISSIN'?

THE VERY ONE.

HE'S ALIVE AND RESPONSIBLE FOR OUR PRESENT *DISASTERS.*

ALL FOR AN ELUSIVE JEWEL KNOWN AS THE *ENIGMATIC PRISM.*

LIGHTBOURNE MURDERED THE FAMED ARCHEOLOGIST *CLIVE PENBERTHY* OVER IT MORE THAN A DECADE AGO.

HE'LL LIKELY *KEEP* KILLING UNTIL HE FINDS IT.

HNHH

I CAN'T... »UHH« LIFT her on my own, PETE. HELP ME... PLEASE.

ANYTHIN' FOR YA, MISS.

SHE'S NOT 'EAVY AT ALL.

THIS ONE'S A SWEET'EART, DOCTOR....

...TAKE GOOD CARE OF 'ER.

PETE, I'VE GOT TO GO...

...OR THERE WILL BE MORE LIKE MICHELLE.

THEN YOU BEST NOT WANDER THESE STREETS ALL BY YER LONESOME.

PETE, I'M FINE...I DON'T NEED AN ESCORT.

PEOPLE OUT THERE NEED YOU.

BUT MIZ EMMA, THE RESIDENCE --

--IS BARELY STANDING.

I SHOULD HAVE EXPECTED AS MUCH.

A RIGHT CHASM, THAT IS.

THAT THE WORD, MIZ EMMA?

YES, PETE...

...THOUGH IT MAY AS WELL BE A *MOAT* AROUND A CASTLE WALL.

CAN WE JUMP IT?

NOT *BLOODY...* AH...I MEAN... *NO*, MISS.

LIKELY SNAP YOUR *LEG* AND SCUFF YOUR PRETTY *KNEES* IN THAT... *CRE-VASSE.*

*H*E TRIES SO HARD, FAILED GENTLEMAN PETE.

TRY AROUND THE *BACK*, MIZ EMMA?

NO, PETE.

IF WE CAN'T ENTER THROUGH THE *FRONT* DOOR...

WE ENTER THROUGH SIMON'S LIBRARY...

...OR MORE PRECISELY, WHAT *REMAINS* OF IT.

WELL, IF ANYTHING...IT'S AN IMPROVEMENT OVER SIMON'S *PREVIOUS* FILING SYSTEM...

...INSCRUTABLE AND *INFURIATING* THOUGH IT WAS.

RRRKKK

PETE!

MIZ EMMA! GRAB HOLD O' *SUMTHIN'!*

...THEN WE'LL JUST HAVE TO FIND OUR OWN MEANS OF *INGRESS*.

COME AGAIN, MISS?

MIND THE KNOTHOLES WITH YOUR PRETTY SHOES, MIZ EMMA.

PETE'S VIGOR AND FIGHTING SPIRIT COULD BE PUT TO BETTER USE THAN LOOSING TIMBERS FOR A MAKESHIFT SPAN.

HANDS, PETE...

SORRY.

GIVEN OUR LUCK IN BESTING MALCOLM LIGHTBOURNE THUS FAR, PERHAPS IT'S HIGH TIME WE CALLED IN *REINFORCEMENTS*...

...IF ONLY TO BOOST MORALE AND BRING UP THE REAR.

GRAB *WHAT*?!

...AS IF AN AVALANCHE OF LEATHER AND PARCHMENT PROVIDES *ANY* PURCHASE OF NOTE.

FBUM

WHULP!

FBUM FBUM FBUM FBUM

WELL, THAT WASN'T *SO* BAD...

I'VE BEEN SEARCHING FOR *THIS* PARTICULAR TREATISE FOR *AGES*.

THERE WAS AN *EASIER* WAY DOWN THE BOOKSHELVES, MIZ EMMA.

OH, I *NEVER* DO THINGS THE EASY WAY, PETE.

IF THE FORENSICS FILES FELL...heh...I'D MOST SURELY BE *SQUASHED.*

IS THEY THE *FOR-EN-SICS* UP THERE?

JUST *A-THROUGH-E*, PETE.

LET'S NOT TEMPT THE *REMAINING* ALPHABET...

I ALWAYS DID FIND LETTERS TO BE *HARD*, MISS.

GOOD ONE, PETE.

DIDJA HEAR THE ONE ABOUT THE BARRISTER AND THE MULE?

THAT'LL DO, PETE.

THE RESIDENCE IS A MAZE OF PASSAGES WHEN IN *GOOD* REPAIR.

NOW WE MUST CONTEND WITH CRUMBLING MORTAR AND DRIZZLING SHARDS OF STAINED GLASS RELEASED FROM THEIR GLAZING IN THE CATHEDRAL'S WINDOWS.

AND THEN THERE IS *OPHELIA*.

WHO?

OPHELIA PRESSMONK, PETE.

OPHELIA, WHAT ARE YOU DOING *HERE?*

WHAT'S HAPPENED TO YOU?

WHAT... WHAT DOES IT *LOOK* LIKE?

I BELIEVE I CAN MAKE THIS LEAP.

GIVE 'ER A RUNNIN' START.

EASY ENOUGH!

PETE, WHAT'S *WRONG?*

IT'S GOOD TO LAUGH AND ALL, 'SPECIALLY *NOW...*

...BUT SHOULDN'T WE HURRY ALONG AND FIND MR. ARCHARD AND THAT *LATEBURN* SOD?

*P*UGILIST PETE, REFUSING TO FIX HIS FIGHTS AND HONEST TO A FAULT.

YOU'RE ABSOLUTELY *RIGHT*, PETE. AFTER ALL I'VE EXPERIENCED IN THE LAST DAYS, I FEEL--

A BIT PUNCH-DRUNK?

IF THAT INCLUDES BEING DASHED AND NEARLY DROWNED, *YES.*

T LOOKS LIKE YOU'VE STUCK YOUR IRSUTE LITTLE CHIN INTO AFFAIRS EST LEFT TO BIGGER FOLKS, OPHELIA.

TOOK A BEATIN' SHE DID. WITH A *STICK*, BY THE LOOKS OF IT.

A CANE.

HE WOULDN'T STOP...HITTING ME...

DO YOU *BLAME* HIM, OPHELIA?

YOU HELPED TO REVEAL MALCOLM LIGHTBOURNE'S ROLE IN THE OXFORD-COLLINS MURDER.

YOU'RE QUITE *LUCKY* HE DIDN'T FINISH YOU OFF OUTRIGHT.

DIDN'T MENTION ANY OF THAT...

KEPT YAPPING ABOUT HIS PRECIOUS *PRISM*...OVER AND OVER.

SAID HE HAD TO SAVE HIS STRENGTH THOUGH...

SAID HE HAD TO LEAVE SOMETHING FOR *SIMON*...

OPHELIA, *WHERE* IS HE? WHERE'S LIGHTBOURNE NOW?

SHE'S OUT, MIZ EMMA. *UN-CON-SCIOUS,* I MEAN.

LITTLE GAL'S BEEN STOMPED GOOD.

BAD, I MEAN.

SHE NEEDS THE ATTENTION OF A *DOCTOR,* PETE.

YOU'RE GOING TO HAVE TO TAKE HER.

AND LEAVE YOU, MISS?

PLEASE, PETE. *FOR* ME.

*I*F THERE WERE TIME FOR REFLECTION I WOULD LIKELY REGRET THAT.

BUT OPHELIA NEEDS PETE AND SIMON NEEDS ME, AND BY THAT ACCOUNTING I AM LEFT TO NAVIGATE THE PITFALLS *ALONE.*

FSSST

OH, DRAT...

THE UPHEAVAL MUST HAVE TWISTED THE GASWORKS OR OVER-TURNED CAUSTIC CHEMICALS IN SIMON'S LABORATORY.

THE STAIRWELL IS A HEAP OF FLAMING RUIN...AND LIGHTBOURNE CAN BE NOWHERE ELSE THAN THE *UPPER* TIERS OF THE RESIDENCE.

BUT HOW CAN I ASCEND--?

THE DUMBWAITER! *PERFECT!*

I DISPEL THE PAIN OF BLISTERS WITH THOUGHTS OF THIS PRISM WHICH DRIVES SIMON AND LIGHTBOURNE TO SUCH *DESPERATION.*

SIMON'S COLLECTION OF VENOMOUS CREEPIES SLITHERS AND SCABBERS FREE OF THEIR TERRARIUM HOMES.

HSSSSSS

SPIDERS AND SNAKES I CAN WEATHER.

MALCOLM LIGHTBOURNE IS A PREDATOR OF AN ENTIRELY *DIFFERENT* ORDER AND PHYLUM.

HE DESIRES ONLY THE ENIGMATIC PRISM...

..AND SIMON'S HEAD *ON A PIKE,* OF COURSE.

I CAN SCARCELY GUESS HOW *MANY* HAVE EXPIRED TO ACHIEVE THE FORMER...

EACH BELIEVES THAT THE OTHER ALREADY *POSSESSES* IT.

AND ONLY *ONE* OF THEM CAN BE CORRECT. BUT IF SO, THEN *WHERE?*

SIMON'S --

-- CANE?

THWUMP

CURIOUS...

...I DON'T RECALL ORDERING *ROOM* SERVICE.

BUT THERE'S *ALWAYS* ROOM FOR JUST DESSERTS, WOT?

SIMON...

WHAT HAS HE *DONE* TO YOU?

Heh... *NICELY DONE, SIMON.*

AND HERE I THOUGHT YOU LEARNED SO VERY LITTLE FROM ME.

MISS BISHOP'S LITTLE PLOY *WON'T* WORK.

SHE...

SHE SPEAKS THE TRUTH, MALCOLM...

NO SHE DOESN'T! WHATEVER *TRUTH* THERE IS TO BE FOUND I'LL BEAT OUT OF HER!

SO FAST...

THE DEEPER HIS RAGE, THE MORE *DANGEROUS* HE BECOMES.

THRAK

STOP THIS!

AND I AM AS GOOD A *TARGET* AS ANY.

HE CAN'T SAVE YOU.

KRINK KRINK

HE *WON'T* SAVE YOU.

KKRINK

SIMON'S DONE FOR. SO ARE *YOU.*

IF I HAVE TO, I'LL SIMPLY WAIT FOR THIS DAMNABLE DOMICILE TO BURN TO THE GROUND AND THEN SIFT THROUGH THE *ASHES.*

I CAN BE *PATIENT.* I'VE DONE IT *BEFORE...*

THEN YOU'RE IN FOR A *LONG* HUNT.

I WON'T SURVIVE THIS.

UNLESS YOU'RE AS GOOD AT ESCAPES AS YOU PROFESS...

...SIMON?

UNHAND HER...

UNFF!

...NOW.

THOK

MALCOLM, WHY IS IT SO *DIFFICULT* FOR YOU TO REALIZE --

--THAT *EVERYTHING* YOU DESIRE WILL ALWAYS SLIP FROM YOUR GRASP?

YOU'VE BEEN HOLDING THE PRISM SINCE YOU FIRST TOOK BACK YOUR CANE IN THE CAVES BENEATH PARTINGTON.

PLINK

THAT'S IT.

THEY DODGE. THEY PARRY. I AM LEFT TO *FEINT*.

YOU CAN STOP THIS NONSENSE!

I'VE GOT THE PRISM!

I'LL STOP WHEN HE'S GOOD AND *DEAD*, MISS BISHOP!

KRAK

UHN!

WELL, WHEN *THAT'S* DONE YOU'LL FIND YOUR ENIGMATIC LITTLE PRISM RIGHT HERE --

--IN SIMON'S THINK-TANK.

SIMON, DO YOU THINK HE *SURVIVED* THE FALL?

HE'S ENDURED *WORSE.*

I *KNOW* HE'S DOWN THERE.

HE'S FAR TOO *CRAFTY* TO DIE.

SHASSSSS

*B*UT STILL...

IT'S QUITE A LONG WAY DOWN.

HE'S FALLEN *FARTHER.*

WE DARE NOT *ASSUME* THAT THIS IS OVER.

WE'LL END IT WITH ROCKS AND CLUBS IF NECESSARY.

BEFORE THIS LUNACY I WOULD HAVE ARGUED CIVILITY OVER VENDETTA.

NOW I SEARCH FOR JUST THE RIGHT BRICK.

GONE.

AGAIN.

YOU MUST BE JOKING.

PLEASE, SIMON...DEVELOP A SENSE OF HUMOR *ANOTHER* DAY.

HE'S ...PPED, ...MMA. AND WITH THE PRISM.

I THOUGHT I COULD **TRUST** YOU NOT TO COMPLICATE MATTERS BEYOND OUR PRESENT WOES.

WHAT? I **SAVED** YOUR **UNGRATEFUL LIFE,** SIMON!

AND YOU FRET OVER THIS-- THIS SIXPENNY **BAUBLE!**

YOU WOULD THINK THAT A MASTER ILLUSIONIST LIKE LIGHTBOURNE WOULD RECOGNIZE SIMPLE SLEIGHT- OF-HAND...FROM A NOVICE, NO LESS.

THE PRISM...

YOU **PALMED** IT AND FEIGNED TOSSING IT INTO THE THINK- TANK.

YES, SIMON.

TRUST IN ME AND YOU'LL FIND THAT I'M **FULL** OF PLEASANT SURPRISES.

I'M **SURPRISED** YOU DIDN'T JUST KEEP THE PRISM TO SATISFY YOUR OWN INEXHAUSTIBLE CURIOUSITY.

WHAT MAKES YOU THINK I **HAVEN'T?**

HE'S ESCAPED, SIMON.

YOU NEEDN'T BOTHER CHANGING THE SUBJECT.

WE'LL ...ATCH HIM ...ANOTHER TIME... ...ANOTHER PLACE.

...N ANY ...VENT, HE ...OULD BE ...SIER TO FIND.

WITH ALL THE OTHER RATS VACATED, MALCOLM LIGHTBOURNE SHOULD STAND OUT LIKE A SORE THUMB.

WAS THAT A **JOKE,** SIMON?

A STATEMENT OF **FACT,** EMMA.

YOU KNOW HUMOR ESCAPES ME **ALSO.**

LOOK WHO IT IS...

WOO! BEEN LOOKIN' EVERYWHERES FOR YA, BOSS!

WAS IT DEM MONKEYS?

I WISH, LAD...

I WISH.

AS DO I, SIMON...

...BUT DESPITE OUR AWKWARD LEVITY, I FEAR WE HAVE LOOSED A MORE **DEADLY** BEAST.

BLOOSH

GLRBLB!

BLBG

BLRG?

I BELIEVE THIS CUDGEL IS WEIGHING YOU **DOWN**.

DO GIVE MY REGARDS TO SIMON, WILL YOU?

WH-WHAT?

NO! YOU CAN'T!

GRLBLB!

STEADY AS SHE GOES, ANTAEUS...

...WE'VE QUITE A LONG JOURNEY AHEAD.

ERRATA

GUICE + MAGYAR + Ponsor

EARLY CLUES

This trade paperback, culled from issues #7-12, marks the second collection of RUSE stories. We pause in retrospect to unveil some of the original unseen artwork that predated the launch of the title. The following offers an exclusive behind-the-scenes look at our colorful cast of characters and unique settings as rendered by the regular RUSE team and a few friendly guest artists.

SIMON AND EMMA

Art by Butch Guice, Rick Magyar and Justin Ponsor

This unpublished piece captures the prevailing attitudes of our intrepid protagonists, if not their "final" look as seen in RUSE today. Emma Bishop, in particular, has evolved slightly, her features now more distinctive from the beauteous blonde sharing the telephone receiver with an apparently pensive Simon Archard.

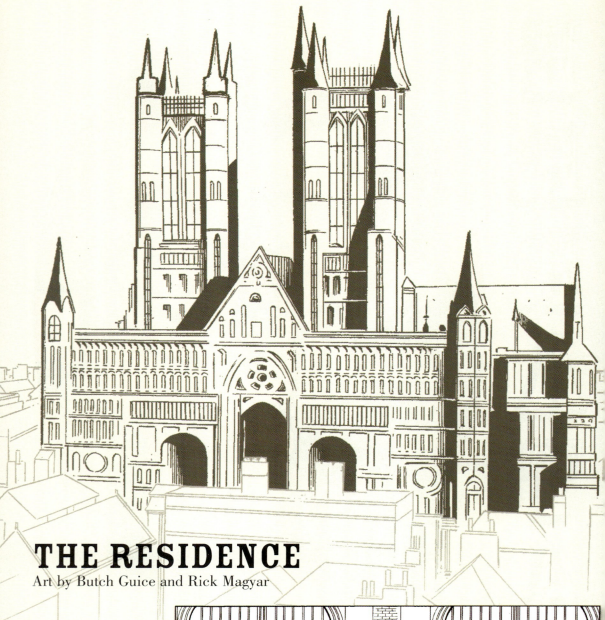

THE RESIDENCE

Art by Butch Guice and Rick Magyar

Only Simon Archard would find an abandoned cathedral to his liking as both home and headquarters. From the cavernous **Study** of the upper Residence, Simon surveys the cobblestone streets of Partington through high, arched windows.

The **Grand Stairwell** further illustrates the sheer immensity of the Residence, corkscrewing up through the center of the cathedral with mysteries and marvels on every floor.

Simon's Library, last seen tumbling in upon itself thanks to Malcolm Lightbourne's "undermining" of Partington, is shown here as it was originally conceived. Taking up an entire wing (and several floors) of the Residence, the Library contains Simon's copious collection of tomes detailing Arcadia's accumulated knowledge of science and sleuthing. Simon eschews alphabetical sorting for his own "system," a code the determined Emma has yet to crack.

Simon's Personal Carriage further illustrates the Victorian atmosphere of RUSE, while offering Partington's "favorite son" a respectable (though seldom seen) mode of transportation throughout the city.

ARCHARD'S AGENTS

Art by Butch Guice, Mike Perkins and Laura DePuy Martin

Some familiar, others not so readily recognizable, Simon's loyal agents from within and without Partington aid our Master Detective with their unique talents, physical, mental, or otherwise.

The diminutive chemist **Otto Pressmonk** was originally to be named Theophilis Bromby. While he met his untimely demise in RUSE: ENTER THE DETECTIVE, his twin sister Ophelia can be seen in this very collection.

Pugilist **Peter Grimes** has become a personal favorite of the creative team, first appearing in ENTER THE DETECTIVE to aid Emma's hunt for a murderous rogue preying on Partington's ladies of the night.

The pouty and brooding **Sarah Athcarne** eventually became our lisping medium Adeline, also first seen in ENTER THE DETECTIVE, but soon to share the RUSE spotlight in her own adventure alongside the simian-challenged "Monkey Boy."

As for Archard's Agents (l. to r.) Nick Scratch, Khartar Singh and Allyn Marsden? Wait and see. Simon's network of sleuthing "seconds" is expansive indeed.

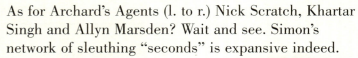

GARGOYLES

Art by Butch Guice, Mike Perkins and Laura DePuy Martin

PECKS

GRYPHS

RAKES

SHIMS

GRONKS

From the beginning, the Victorian atmosphere of RUSE is made more uniquely "otherworldly" with the addition of Partington's ubiquitous Gargoyle population, appearing here in all its winged diversity from tiny Pecks to more massive Gronks, birdlike Gryphs (after the mythical "gryphon" or "griffin") and Shims, and devilish Rakes, perhaps most resembling our conception of the ledge-perching creatures. Where did the Gargoyles originate? How did Partington become home to these seemingly benign beasties? The answers to these and other mysteries are forthcoming in the pages of RUSE.

MIRANDA'S HENCHMEN

Art by Butch Guice, Mike Perkins and Laura DePuy Martin

Readers of this RUSE collection can spy the return of the ruthless Baroness Miranda Cross in the closing pages of our epic story. Interestingly, Miranda's omnipresent henchman Antaeus — whose sheer size precludes him fitting inside a standard comic book panel — wasn't the original choice to aid and abet our fetching femme fatale. Even before the first issue of RUSE saw print, one idea had Miranda commanding a cadre of her own criminal-minded agents mutated from Partington's various Gargoyle sub-species. Included here are four such unseen henchmen, preliminary names and gargoyle beginnings attached.

SKYRNE (SHIM)

HOBBS (GRYPH)

WITHERS (PECK)

BACCHUS (GRONK)

CROSSGEN COMICS®
GRAPHIC NOVELS

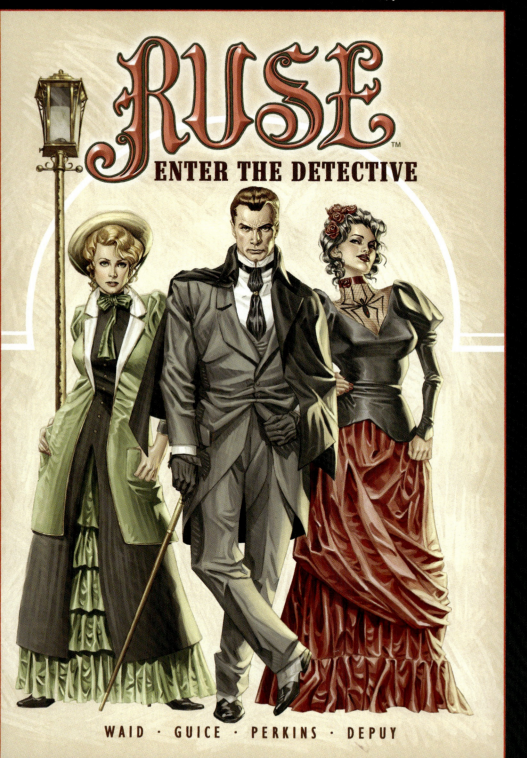